NEET
Imperative
ZOOLOGY (XI)

(An accomplished guide for NEET aspirants)

- **NCERT based concept**
- **Golden points**
- **Knowledge Points**
- **Multiple choice questions (MCQs)**
- **Assertion & Reason questions**

Author

Dr. Pradeep Kumar Maharana

AF795859

Preface

I feel an immense pleasure to present my book entitled **"NEET Imperative ZOOLOGY (XI)"** based on latest NCERT syllabus. This book will help students, who are preparing for NEET and also quite helpful for class XI students. Every NEET aspirants can easily understand the basic concept of zoology at NCERT level.
The basic features of this book are given below:

- Easy notes with quick understanding based on NCERT concept.
- Unique questions with explanations are also included in Golden point.
- Additional terms and concepts are also included in Knowledge points.
- Chapter wise difference between are included.
- Chapter wise objective type questions are also included.
- Chapter wise assertion and reason questions are also included.

Reader's views are welcome. I request the readers, to send their queries, suggestion or criticism on this book. So that I can improve and serve you better.

Dr Pradeep Kumar Maharana

Emai ID: www.pradeepmaharana@gmail.com

Acknowledgements

I thank almighty Lord Jagannath who gave me this opportunity to complete this book. The blessings of my parents have a prime role in making me more determined and focused towards my goal. My wife and other family members inspired me throughout the preparation of this book.

Dr Pradeep Kumar Maharana

Contents

Sl No.	CONTENTS	Page Numbers
1	**Chapter-1: Animal Kingdom**	1 - 21
2	**Chapter-2: Structural organization in animals (Animal tissue, Cockroach & Frog)**	22 - 41
3	**Chapter-3: Breathing and exchange of gases**	42 - 57
4	**Chapter-4: Body fluid and circulation**	58 - 75
5	**Chapter-5: Excretory products and their Elimination**	76 - 89
6	**Chapter-6: Locomotion and movement**	90 - 105
7	**Chapter-7: Neural control and Coordination**	106 - 119
8	**Chapter-8: Chemical Coordination and Integration**	120 - 136
9	**Chapter-9: Biomolecules**	137 - 152
10	**Answer Key for chapter wise MCQs and Assertion & Reason questions**	153 - 156

Chapter-1: ANIMAL KINGDOM

- **Fundamental features of animals**
- **Nonchordates**
- **Chordates**
- **Golden Box**
- **Knowledge points**
- **Multiple choice questions (MCQs)**
- **Assertion & Reason questions**

FUNDAMENTAL FEATURES OF ANIMALS:

More than one million of animal species have been described till date. The fundamental features of animals include arrangement of cells, symmetry of body, coelom, digestive, circulatory or reproductive systems.

Level of organisation

Animals (multicellular) show different pattern of organization.

a) *Cellular level of organisation*: loose arrangement of cells (sponges)
b) *Tissue level of organisation*: Here group of cells have same functions (coelenterates)
c) *Organ level of organisation*: Here organs are present (Platyhelminthes)
d) *Organ system level of organisation*: Here organs are associated with functional systems (from Aschehelmithes to chordates)

Symmetry:

a) ***Asymmetry*:** Here organism body cannot divide into equal halves (sponges).
b) ***Radial symmetry*:** Here plane passed through central axis of body and divide the organisms into two equal halves (Cnidaria, ctenophore, adult stage of echinodermata)
c) ***Bilateral symmetry*:** Here one plane of axis is present and divide the organism into two equal halves (From platyhelminthes to chordates)

Germ layers: *(figure-1)*

Two germ layers / embryonic layers *(a)* i.e. ectoderm and endoderm are present in diploblastic organisms (Cnidaria and ctenophore). Three germ layers *(b)* i.e. ectoderm, endoderm and mesoderm are present in triploblastic organisms (Platyhelminthes to chordates).

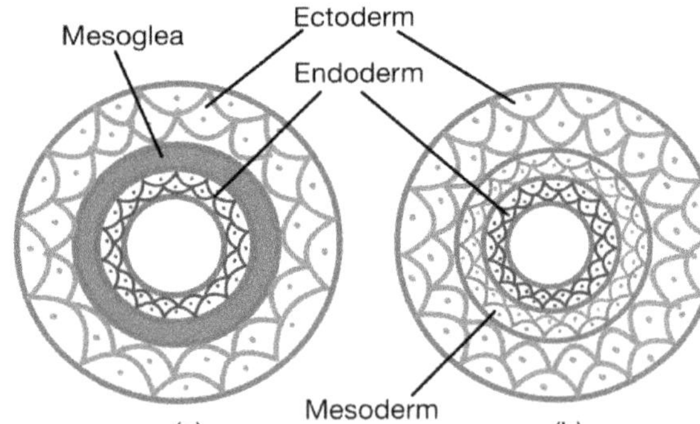

Figure-1: (a) Two germ layers (b) Three germ layers

Coelom:

The cavity in between gut and body wall is called as coelom. This body cavity should be lined with mesoderm. Acoelomates are the animals (platyhelminthes) in which body cavity is absent. In some case, mesoderm is present in scattered pouches that means body cavity is not lined with

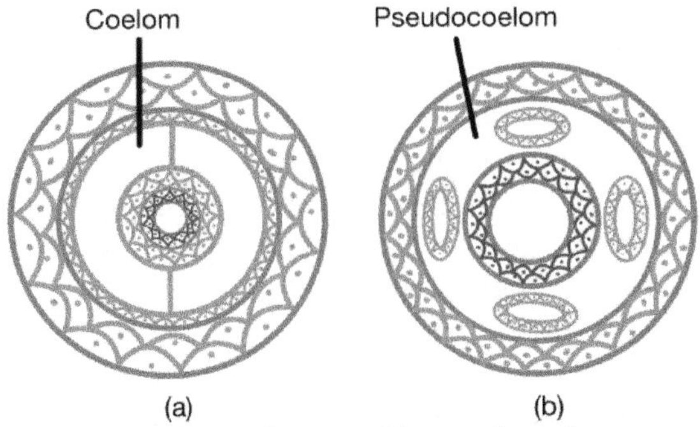

Figure-2: (a) Coelomate, (b) Pseudocoelomate

mesoderm and the animals (ascehelminthes) are called as pseudooelomates *(figure-2, b)*. Annelids, arthropods, mollusks, echinoderms hemochordata and chordates are belongs to coelomates *(figure-2, a)*.

Segmetation

In metameric segmentation, body is internally and externally divided into segments.

Notochord: It is mesodermal in origin and form rod like structure on dorsal side during embryonic development. On the basis of presence or absence of notochord, animals are categorized into chordates and non chordates (e.g. porifera to echinoderms).

GOLDEN BOX-1:

If the fundamental features of animals are not considered, then what are the problems we will face during the classification of animals?

If the common features are not in consideration, then classification becomes inconsistent. Again, it is difficult to determine evolutionary relationship and harder to understand biological information globally.

Write down the steps to classify a given specimen?

The initial observations for the classification of a novel species are microscopic features, behavior or movement and habitat. Again that species should be compared with known species on the basis of taxonomical background. Again, we should follow the ecological role, phylogenetic relationship and genetic analysis of that species.

Coelom (body cavity) is useful in animal classification. Explain it?

In animal classification, the nature of the body cavity and coelom is one of the fundamental and informative systems of animal taxonomy. It reveals development and structural pattern of animals, helps in grouping of animals, support functional and anatomical comparison among animals and represent evolutionary advancement. So it is highly significant.

NONCHODATES:

Porifera (sponges):

They are the sponges and generally marine in habitat. Their basic characterstics are cellular level of organisation, asymmetry (mostly) and cellular type of body plan. Canal system is the specialised characters of porifera. Here water enters into spongocoel (central cavity) through ostia (minute pores) and removed out from the body through ***osculum***. Spongocoel is lined with choanocytes or collar cells.

Its physiological characters includes

a) Intracellular digestion
b) Both respiration and excretion takes place through the pathway of water transport
c) ***Spicules*** and ***sponging fibres*** are the skeletal structures.
d) Reproduction is asexual (fragmentation) and sexual (formation of gametes) type
e) They are hermaphrodite and show the characteristics of internal fertilisation and indirect developmemt.

Examples: Scypha or sycon, Euspongia or bath sponge and Spongilla or fresh water sponges.

Coelenterata (Cnidaria) *(figure-3)*:

Figure-3: Aurelia

They are aquatic (mostly marine) in habitat and show the characteristics of sessile or free swimming. Tissue level of organisation, diploblastic, gastro-vascular cavity with hypostome, ***Cnidoblast*** or ***Cnidocytes*** present in tentacles and contain nematocyst (stinging capsule). Cnidoblasts are used for anchorage, defence and capture of prey. Medusa (umbrella shaped, free swimming, e.g. Aurelia or jelly fish) and polyp (cylindrical shaped, sessile, e.g. Hydra, Adamsia) are two basic form of cnidarians.

The physiological characters includes

a) Digestion is extracellular and intracellular.
b) Respiration and excretion takes place through body surface.
c) Some cnidaria (like obelia) show the characteristics of alteration of generation (metagenesis). Polyp (cylinder like) give medusa (umbrella like) asexually and medusa form polyps sexually.
d) Some cnidarians (corals) have skeleton which is consisting of calcium carbonate.

Examples: Portuguese man of war (physalia), Sea anemone (Adamsia), Sea pen (Pennatula), Sea fan (gorgonian) and Brain coral (Meandrina).

Ctenophora (Sea walnuts or comb jellies):

They are exclusively marine in habitat and show the characteristics of tissue level of organisation, radial symmetry, diploblastic, blind sac etc. Eight external rows of ciliated comb plates are present which are responsible for locomotion. This group of organisms has ***bioluminescence*** characteristics (capable to emit light).

The physiological characters includes

a) Digestion is both extracellular and intracellular
b) Both respiration and excretion takes place through body surface.
c) Hermaphrodite and sexual reproduction
d) Fertilisation is external and development is indirect

Examples: Pleurobrachia and ctenoplana

Platyhelmithes (flatworms):

They are mostly endoparasites and dorsoventrally flattened. They show the characteristics of organ level of organisation, bilateral symmetry, triploblastic, blind sac and acoelomates. ***Hooks*** and ***suckers*** are the special characters of parasitic form. Some members have the capacity of regeneration. The physiological characters includes

a) Nutrients are absorbed through general body surface.
b) Respiration takes place through general body surface
c) Excretion takes place through flame cells (also responsible for osmoregulation)
d) Sexual dimorphism, fertilisation is internal, development through many larval stages

Examples: Tapeworm (Taenia), Liver fluke (Fasciola).

Aschelmithes (Roundworms):

They are free living, aquatic, terrestrial or parasitic in plants and animals. They show the characterstics of organ system level of organisation, bilateral symmetry, triploblastic, tube within tube (protostomic type), pseudocoelomate.

The physiological characters include:

a) Complete alimentary canal with ***muscular pharynx***
b) Respiration takes place through body surface. Body waste are removed from excretory tube through excretory pore
c) Sexes are separate (dioecious), female are longer than male.
d) Fertlisation is internal and development may be direct or indirect.

Examples: Ascaris (Roundworm), Wuchereria (Filaria worm), Ancylostoma (Hookworm).

GOLDEN BOX-2:

How intracellular digestion is different from extracellular digestion?

Intracellular digestion is different from extracellular digestion on the basis of location, secretion of enzymes, and availability in organisms. In intracellular type, digestion is taking place inside cell, where enzymes are secreted into vacuoles or lysosome. This type is more common in unicellular organisms (Amoeba). In extracellular type, digestion is taking place outside cells (in tube or cavity). Extracellular digestion is common in multicellular organisms (like humans, fungi etc.).

Explain the difference between direct and indirect development?

Development is categorized into direct and indirect development on the basis of larval stage, resemblance to adult and metamorphosis. In direct development, young are resembles with adult. Here larval stage is absent. So metamorphosis does not take place. In Indirect development, young's are different from adult. Here larval stage is present. So metamorphosis takes place.

Find out the specific features of platyhelminthes?

The peculiar features of parasitic platyhelminthes are Dorso-ventrally flattened, Presence of hooks and suckures, It completes its life cycle through two or more hosts., They have specialised forms of larval stages

Write down the list of animals that are parasitic to human beings?

Tapeworm (*Taenia solium*; It is the intestinal parasite), **Roundworm** (*Ascaris lumbricoides*; It lives in intestine and causes malnutrition), **Hookworm** (*Ancylostoma duodenale*; It enters body through skin and feed on blood in intestine), **Pinworm** (*Enterobius vermicularis*; It is common in children and causing itching around the anus), **Liverfluke** (*Fasciola hepatica*; It will affect liver and bile ducts), **Filaria worm** (*Wuchereria bancrofti;* It is also called as Filariasis or elephantiasis, Transmitted by culex mosquito, affect lymphatic regions).

Annelida *(figure-4)***:**

They are free living, aquatic (marine or fresh water) or terrestrial. Sometimes they are parasitic. The basic characteristics are organ system level of organisation, bilateral symmetry, triploblastic, segmented (metameric

Figure-4: Earthworm

segmentation) and coelomate. Both longitudinal and circular muscles are present, which helps in locomotion. Parapodia (present in aquatic annelids like Nereis) is the lateral appendages which helps in swimming.
The physiological characters include:

a) Digestion is complete, cutaneous respiration
b) Excretion takes place through ***nephridia*** (also responsible for osmoreguation)
c) Closed type of circulation
d) Paired ganglia, lateral nerves and double ventral nerve code are the component of neural sytem.
e) Sexual reproduction, Dioecious (Nereis aquatic), Monoecious (earthworm and leech)

Examples: Earthworm (Pheretima), Nereis, Leech (Hirudinaria).

Arthropoda (largest phylum of arthropoda)**:**
It occupies about 2/3rd population of all animals. Organ system level of organisation, bilateral symmetry, triploblastic, segmented, tube within tube (protostomic) and coelomate are the basic characteristics of arthropoda.
Head, thorax and abdomen are the major component. Chitinous exoskeleton is the covering of this group of organisms.
The physiological characters include:

a) Digestion is complete. Respiration takes place through gills or book gills or book lungs or tracheal system.
b) Open type circulatory system. Excretion is generally takes place through malpighian tubules (insects).
c) Eyes (compound and simple), antennae, statocyst (balancing organs) are the sense organs.
d) Reproduction is sexual, dioecious, internal fertilisation, mostly oviparous and development is direct or indirect.

Examples: Honey bee (Apis), Silkworm (Bombyx), Lac insects (Laccifer] is the economic important insects. Anopheles, Aedes and culex mosquitoes are considered as vectors. Locust or locusta is gregarious pest. Limulus or king crab is living fossils. Other examples are moth, scorpion and prawn.

Figure-5: Snail

Mollusca (second largest phylum) *(figure-5)***:**
They are aquatic (fresh water or marine) or terrestrial in habitat. The basic characteristics include organ system level of organisation, bilateral symmetry, triploblastic, coelomate,

unsegmented etc. Head, muscular foot and visceral hump are the components of mollusks. Calcareous shell covers the body. ***Mantle*** is a soft and spongy and present above visceral hump. Mantle cavity is the space in between hump and mantle.
The physiological characters include:

a) Digestion is complete. ***Radula*** (file like rasping organ) present in mouth.
b) Both respiration and excretion takes place through feathers like gills.
c) Reproduction is sexual type. Dioecious, oviparous and indirect developments are other characteristics.

Examples: Pearl oyster (pinctaada), cuttlefish (sepia), squid (loligo), Devil fish or octopus, Sea hare (Aplysia), Tusk shell (Dentallium), chiton (Chaeloptopleura), Apple snail or Pila.

GOLDEN BOX-3:

The character segmentation is first observed in which group of animal kingdom?

Annelida

Arthropods are the largest group of animal kingdom, Explain it?

On the basis of species diversity and numbers, arthropods are the largest groups in animal kingdom. Again, arthropods have features like ecological flexibility (found in nearly all ecosystems), reproductive strategies (produce large number of offsprings & rapid evolution in short duration of time), and morphological innovation (small body size helps organisms to live in tiny niche and diverse habitat) and evolutionary history existed over 500 million years. So they are well adapted to the environment of earth than others.

Water vascular system belongs to which group of animal kingdom?

Echinodermata

Figure-6: Starfish

Echinodermata (spiny bodies) *(figure-6)*:
They are exclusively marine in habitat. The basic characteristics includes organ system level of organisation, Radial symmetry (adult) and bilateral symmetry (larva), triploblastic, coelomates, tube within tube (dueterostomic)..
The physiological characters include:

a) Digestive system is complete. Here, mouth is ventral and anus is dorsal.

b) ***Water vascular system*** is present which helps in locomotion, capturing and transportation of food. No excretory system.
c) Sexual reproduction, sexual dimorphism, Fertilization is usually external and development is indirect.

Examples: Star fish or Asterias, Sea urchin (Echinus), Sea lilly (Antedon), Sea cucumber (Cucumaria) and Brittle star or Ophiura.

Hemichordata: They are worm like marine animals and belong to nonchordates. Here rudimentary structure i.e. ***stomochord*** (similar to notochord) is present at collar region.

Organ system level of organization, bilateral symmetry, triploblastic, coelomate, tube within tube (dueterostomic) is also the basic characteristics of this group of organisms. Body is consisting of proboscis, a collar and trunk.

The physiological characteristics are as follows.

a) Digestion is complete and Respiration takes place through gills
b) Excretion takes place through proboscis gland and circulation is open type.
c) Reproduction is sexual type, sexual dimorphism, external Fertilisation and indirect development

Examples: Balanoglossus, saccoglossus

Nonchordates	Characteristics	Examples
1) Porifera	Asymmetrical, pores on body, no true tissues or organs	Sponges (e.g., *Sycon*)
2) Cnidaria	Radial symmetry, tentacles with stinging cells (cnidocytes), body forms: polyp/medusa	Jellyfish, Hydra, Sea anemone
3) Ctenophora	Radial symmetry, bioluminescent, comb plates for movement	Comb jellies
4) Platyhelminthyes	Bilateral symmetry, flat body, no body cavity (acoelomate), parasitic or free-living	Tapeworm, Planaria
5) Aschelminthes	Bilateral symmetry, round body, pseudocoelomate, parasitic/free-living	Ascaris, Hookworm
6) Annelida	Segmented body, true coelom, closed circulatory system	Earthworm, Leech

7) Arthropoda	Segmented body, jointed limbs, exoskeleton of chitin, most diverse group	Insects, Spider, Crab
8) Mollusca	Soft body, often with hard shell, muscular foot, mantle	Snail, Octopus, Mussel
9) Echinodermata	Radial symmetry (in adults), spiny skin, water vascular system	Starfish, Sea urchin
10) Hemichordata	Worm like, dueterostomic, presence of proboscis gland	Balanoglossus, saccoglossus

CHORDATES:

Presence of notochord, dorsal nerve cord (single and hollow), pharyngeal gill slits (paired) are the fundamental characters of chordates.

The basic characteristics of chordates includes organ system level of organization, bilateral symmetry, triploblastic, coelomates (enterocoelic), tube within tube (dueterostomic). Presence of post anal tail and closed type circulation are also the characteristics of chordates.

Urochordates, Cephalochordates and Vertebrata are the three subphyla of chordates. Here urochordates and cephalochordates are referred to as protochordates (exclusively marine).

a) In Urochordates (Tunicates), notochord is only present in larval tail region. Here ***retrogressive metamorphosis*** takes place. Examples: Ascidia, salpa, Doliolum
b) In Cephalochordates, notochord present in head initially and later extends towards the tail region and persists throughout their life.

Examples: Branchiostoma (Amphioxus or Lancelet).

Vertebrata:

In this group, notochord (in embryonic period) is replaced by vertebral column (in adult). Here vertebral column is made up cartilage or bone. Vertebrata contains all basic characters of chordates. Besides this, it shows the characteristics of ventral heart (two, three or four chambers), paired appendages (either fins or limbs) and kidneys (for excretion and osmoregulation).

Cyclostomata (circular mouth without jaws) **:**

They are marine in habitat and their bodies are elongated. They are ectoparasites on some fishes. Cyclostomata migrate to fresh water for spawning purposes and become dead within few days.

a) Here cranium and vertebral column are made up cartilage.
b) Gill slits (6 to 15 pairs) are present, which helps in respiration. Circulation is closed type

c) Here scales and paired fins are absent

Examples: Lamprey or Petromyzon, Hagfish (Myxine).

Chondrichthyes *(figure-7)*:

Figure-7: Shark

They are predaceous and marine in habitat. Body is streamlined and endoskeleton is made up cartilage. They are poikilothermous and cannot regulate their body temperature. Here notochord is persisting throughout life. Constantly, they swim in water to avoid sinking due to absence of air bladder. Skin (tough) contains minute ***placoid scales***.

a) Mouth is ventral in position and their jaws are very powerful.
b) Gill slits are separate. Here operculum (gill cover) is absent. Two chambered heart.
c) Claspers are present in pelvic fins of male. Sexes are separated, fertilisation internal and many of them are viviparous.
d) Some have electric organs (Torpedo) and some posses poison sting (Trygon).

Examples: Dog fish or scoliodon, Saw fish or Pristis, Great white shark (Carcharodon), Sting ray (Trygon),

Osteichthyes:

They are either marine or fresh water in habitat and have streamline body. Here endoskeleton is made up bone. They are poikilothermous.

Mouth is terminal (mostly). They have 4 pairs of gills and covered by operculum. Heart is two chambered (one auricle and one ventricle). Here ***cycloid/ctenoid scales*** are present on skin and air bladder regulates buoyancy.

Sexes are separate, usually external fertlisation, mostly oviparous and development is direct.

Examples: Flying fish (Exocoetus), Sea horse (Hippocampus), Rohu (labeo), Katla (Catla), Magur (Clarias), Fighting fish (Betta), Angle fish (Pterophyllum). Rohu, Katla, Magur are fresh water; while Betta and Pterophyllum are aquarium.

Amphibia (both aquatic as well as terrestrial):

They are cold blooded animals. Body is divisible into head and trunk. But in some case, tail is present. Skin is moist. Scales are absent. Eyelids and tympanum are present.

Respiration takes place through gills, lungs and skin. Heart is 3 chambered. Cloaca is present (connection of alimentary canal, urinary and reproductive tracts)

Sexes are separate. Fertilisation is external. Development is indirect. They are oviparous

Examples: Toad (Bufo), Frog or Rana, Tree frog (Hyla), Salamander, Limbless amphibians (Ichthyophis).

GOLDEN BOX-4:

Why all vertebrates are considered chordates but its vice-versa is not considered?

During embryonic development, all the chordate characters are present in vertebrates. But some chordates like urochoradata and cephalochordata do not have vertebral column. So the statement is right.

Explain the important of air bladder in Pisces?

In most bony fishes, gas filled sac i.e. air bladder is present. It maintains buoyancy without expending energy and adjusts the gas in bladder to ascend or descend in water. That means air bladder allows efficient energy conservation during resting or slow movements. Fish need to be swim constantly without airbladder. Otherwise fish will sink.

Explain the modified characters of birds that help in flying?

Pneumatic bones (hollow with air spaces) are present in birds and reduce its weight without decrease in its strength. Birds have air sacs (respiratory adaptation), which helps in continuous unidirectional air flow through lungs. Again birds have powerful flight muscles. Besides this, they have flight features (provide lift and thrust), large heart related to body size (support high metabolic rate to sustain flight). These are the modifications through which helps birds to fly.

Is it possible that the numbers of eggs produced by oviparous is equal to the numbers of young ones in viviparous mothers?

If the numbers of eggs or young individuals produced from oviparous or viviparous mothers are equal. Then it will be a coincidence. Because both reproductive and survival strategies are different in both the animals.

Reptilia (creep or crawling) *(figure-8)*:

They are mostly terrestrial in habitat and poikilothermous. Dry and cornified skin, epidermal scales or scutes are present in body surface.

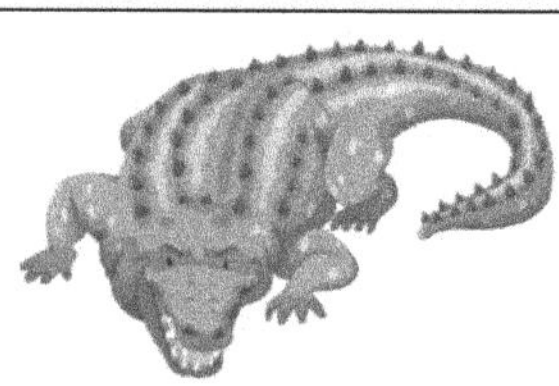

Figure-8: Crocodile

a) No external ear openings. Tympanum is present. Three chambered heart, but in case crocodile, it is 4 chambered.
b) In Reptiles like snakes lizards, casting of skin scales takes place.
c) Sexes are separated. Fertilisation is internal. The development indirect, oviparous

Figure-9: Penguin

Examples: Turtle or Chelone, Tree lizard or Chameleon, Garden lizard (Calotes), Crocodile or Crocodilus, Alligator, wall lizard (Hemidactylus), Cobra or Naja, Krait (bangarus), Viper.

Aves (presence of feathers) *(figure-9)*:

They are warm blooded animals. Here wings are the modification of forelimbs. Scales are present in hindlimbs. Oil glands are present at the base of tail and skin become dry due to absence of glands. Hind limbs help in walking, swimming or clasping the tree branches. Endoskeleton is made up bone and called as ***pneumatic bone*** due to presence of air cavities. Here beak is also present. The physiological characteristics include:

a) Digestion is complete. Crop and gizzard are associated with digestive tract.
b) Four chambered heart and respiration takes place through lungs. Here air sacs are connected to lungs.
c) Sexes are separated, Oviparous, fertilisation internal and development is direct.

Examples: Crow (Corvus), Pigeon (Columba), Parrot or Psittacula, Ostrich or Struthio, peacock or Pavo, Penguin (Aptenodytes), Vulture or Neophron.

Mammalia *(figure-10)*:

They nourish their young ones due to presence of mammary glands and have variety of habitat like forests, dark caves, mountains, desearts, ice caps etc. They are homoithermous and have different types of teeth in jaws. Besides this, two pairs of limbs (for walking, climbing, swimming, flying, running etc.), external ear (pinnae), and hairs on its body surface are also present.

Figure-10: Blue whale

a) Respiration takes place through lungs and heart is four chambered.
b) Sexes are separated, fertilisation is internal, viviparous and development is direct.

Examples: Platypus or Ornithorhynchus, Kangaroo or Macropus, Flying fox or Pteropus, Camel (Camelus), Tiger (Pathera tigris), Lion (Pathera leo), Blue whale or Balaenoptera, Dolphin (Delphinus), Horse (Equus), Elephant (Elephas), Cat (Felis), Dog (Canis), Rat (rattus), Monkey (Macaca).

Chordates	Characteristics	Examples
1) Urochodrates	Notochord in larval stage only, marine, sac-like body	Ascidia, Salpa, Doliolum
2) Cephalochordates	Notochord throughout life, fish-like body, no head	Amphioxus (Lancelet)
3) Cyclostomata	Jawless, circular mouth, parasitic or scavengers	Lamprey, Hag fish
4) Chondroichtyces	Notochord persists throughout life; Air bladder & operculum absent, Claspers present in male, Placoid scales are present. Many are viviparous	Dog fish, Saw fish, Carcardon, Sting ray
5) Osteoichthyoces	Presence of cycloid/ctenoid scales and air bladder. Mostly oviparous.	Clarias, Betta, Pterophyllum, Exocoetus, Hippocampus
6) Amphibia	Life in land and water, moist skin, respiration through gills (in larva), lungs & skin, cloaca present.	Bufo, Rana, Hyla, Salamander, Ichthyophis
7) Reptilia	Dry scaly skin, cold-blooded, lay shelled eggs	Chelone, Calotes, Hemidactylus, Bangarus
8) Aves	Presence of feathers and beak, warm-blooded, flight (mostly), lay eggs	Corvus, Psittacula, Aptenodytes, Neophron

9) Mammals	Presence of mammary glands and hairs, warm-blooded, viviparous (mostly)	Ornithorhynchus, Pteropus, Camelus, Macaca

DIFFERENCE BETWEEN:

Non-chordates	Chordates
i. Notochord is absent ii. Nerve cord is double, solid and ventral. iii. Post-anal tail is absent. iv. Pharyngeal gill slits are absent. v. Heart is dorsal vi. Mostly bilateral symmetry. Some show radial symmetry.	i. Notochord is present at embryonic stage or replaced by vertebral column. ii. Nerve cord is single, hollow and dorsal. iii. Post-anal tail is present in some stage of life iv. Pharyngeal gill slits are present. v. Heart is ventral. vi. It shows bilateral symmetry.

KNOWLEDGE POINTS:

- Cnidarians are economically, environmentally, and biologically important.
- ***Ascaris, Pinworms, Trichinella, Hookworms*** etc. are the roundworms. Ascaris can produce 2 lakhs eggs per day and can survive upto months or years in soil. Pinworm (Enterobius) hatches in duodenum and mature in large intestine. Trichinella are viviparous and burrow in mucous of small intestine of host. This parasite can penetrate skeletal muscle and known as largest intracellular parasite.

  Hookworms are dorsally curved at its anterior end and present at intestine and suck blood. Hookworm diseases are responsible for mental retardation, loss of energy in children.
- ***Leech*** has both anterior and posterior suckers. Here clitellum is present and coelom is packed with connective tissue and muscle.

- ❖ ***Insect*** is the largest class of arthropoda. Many insects are carrier of diseases and feed crop plants. Insects help in pollination of food crop plants.
- ❖ Cephalopoda (complex mollusks) are predators and have suckers in their tentacles.
- ❖ Hemichordates have ***buccal diverticulum*** and show affinity with echinoderms and chordates.
- ❖ Many fishes are migratory and have strategies for their sexual reproduction. Most Fishes are oviparous
- ❖ The eggs of all amphibians need cool and moist environment.
- ❖ Snakes have highly kinetic skull which helps in swallowing of prey larger than snake own diameter. Snakes have weak visual and auditory senses. But snake depends upon chemical senses (***Jacobson's organ***) to hunt the prey. Again pits viper use infrared sensing organ to track warm bodied prey.
- ❖ Birds have poor sense of smell, but they have keen eyesight, good hearing capacity and great coordination of flight. Some birds are flightlessness and found in islands where terrestrial predators are absent.
- ❖ Mammals are ***monotremes*** (egg laying mammals), ***marsupials*** (have mothers pouch where young one is cared) and ***eutherians*** (Placental mammals). Here marsupials and eutherians are viviparous.

MULTIPLE CHOICE QUESTIONS (MCQ)-1:

1. Which cells line the spongocoel in Poriferans ?
(a) Mesenchymal cells
(b) Ostia
(c) Choanocytes
(d) Oscula

2. Which of the following is not a characteristic of the phylum Arthropoda?
(a) Jointed appendages
(b) Metameric segmentation
(c) Chitinous exoskeleton
(d) Parapodia

3. This is an example of bilaterally symmetrical and triploblastic animal
(a) Sponges
(b) Cnidarians
(c) Ctenophores

(d) Round worms

4. Phylum Annelida is not characterized by

(a) Ventral nerve chord
(b) Segmentation
(c) Closed circulatory system
(d) Pseudocoelom

5. Which of the following contains notochord in the embryonic stage?

(a) Non-chordates
(b) Vertebrates
(c) Some of the chordates
(d) All chordates

6. Find the characteristic feature, which is present only in the phylum Coelenterata is

(a) Nematocysts
(b) Hermaphroditism
(c) Polymorphism
(d) Flame cells

7. Excretion is performed by ________ in flatworms.

(a) Protonephridia
(b) Flame cells
(c) Malpighian tubules
(d) Green glands

8. Tube feet are found in

(a) Jellyfish
(b) Cuttlefish
(c) Crayfish
(d) Starfish

MULTIPLE CHOICE QUESTIONS (MCQ)-2

1. Metagenesis refers to
   (a) Occurrence of a drastic change in form during post-embryonic development.
   (b) Presence of a segmented body and parthenogenetic mode of reproduction.
   (c) Presence of different morphic forms.
   (d) Alternation of generation between asexual and sexual phases of an organism.
2. A jawless fish, which lays eggs in fresh water and whose ammocoetes larvae after metamorphosis return to the ocean is

(a) Myxine
(b) Neomyxine
(c) Petromyzon
(d) Eptatretus

3. Body having meshwork of cells, internal cavities lined with food filtering flagellated cells and indirect developments are the characteristics of phylum
   (a) Porifera
   (b) Protozoa
   (c) Coelenterata
   (d) Mollusca
4. Which of the following features is not present in the Phylum – Arthropoda?
   (a) Jointed appendages
   (b) Chitinous exoskeleton
   (c) Metameric segmentation
   (d) Parapodia
5. Which of the following characteristic features always holds true for the corresponding group of animals?
   (a) Cartilaginous endoskeleton – Chondrichthyes
   (b) 3-chambered heart with one incompletely divided ventricle. – Reptilia
   (c) Possess a mouth with an upper and a lower jaw – Chordata
   (d) Viviparous – Mammalia
6. Which of the following are correctly matched with respect to their taxonomic classification?
   (a) Centipede, millipede, spider, scorpion Insecta
   (b) Flying fish, cattle fish, silverfish, Pisces
   (c) House fly, butterfly, tsetse fly, silverfish Insecta
   (d) Spiny anteato, sea urchin, sea cucumber echinodermata
7. Which group of animals belongs to the same phylum?
   (a) Earthworm, Pinworm, Tapeworm
   (b) Malaria parasite, Amoeba, Mosquito
   (c) Prawn, Scorpion, Locusta
   (d) Sponge, Sea anemone, Starfish
8. One of the representatives of Phylum Arthropoda is
   (a) Cuttle fish
   (b) Silver fish
   (c) Flying fish
   (d) Puffer fish

9. Select the Taxon mentioned that represent both marine and fresh water species:
   (a) Cephalochordata
   (b) Echinoderms
   (c) Ctenophora
   (d) Cnidaria
10. Which one of the following statements about all the four of Spongilla, leech, dolphin and penguin is correct?
   (a) Leech is a fresh water form while all others are marine in habitat.
   (b) Penguin is homoiothermic while the remaining three are poikilothermic.
   (c) Spongilla has special collared cells called choanocytes, not found in the remaining three.
   (d) All are bilaterally symmetrical.
11. Which one of the following kinds of animals are triploblastic?
   (a) Flat worms
   (b) Corals
   (c) Sponges
   (d) Ctenophores
12. Which one of the following statements about certain given animals is correct?
   (a) Flat worms (Platyhelminthes) are coelomates
   (b) Round worms (Aschelminthes) are pseudocoelomates
   (c) Molluscs are acoelomates
   (d) Insects are pseudocoelomates
13. Which one of the following statements is totally wrong about the occurrence of notochord, while the other three are correct?
   (a) It is replaced by a vertebral column in adult frog.
   (b) It is present only in larval tail in ascidian.
   (c) It is absent throughout life in humans from the very beginning.
   (d) It is present throughout life in Amphioxus.
14. Frogs differ from humans in possessing
   (a) Hepatic portal system
   (b) Paired cerebral hemispheres
   (c) Nucleated red blood cells
   (d) Thyroid as well as parathyroid
15. What will you look for to identify the sex of the following?

(a) Female cockroach – Anal cerci
(b) Male frog – A copulatory pad on the first digit of the hind limb
(c) Male shark – Claspers borne on pelvic fin
(d) Female ascaris – Sharply curved posterior end

ASSERTION AND REASON QUESTIONS:

Read the **assertion** *and* **reason** *carefully to mark the correct option out of the options given below:*

(a) If both the assertion and the reason are true and the reason is a correct explanation of the assertion.
(b) If both the assertion and reason are true but the reason is not a correct explanation of the assertion.
(c) If the assertion is true but the reason is false.
(d) If both the assertion and reason are false.

1. **Assertion:** Metameric segmentation present in annelids.
   Reason: Both external as well as internal division takes place in annelids body.
2. **Assertion:** Platyhelminthes have flattened body structure and called as flat worms.
   Reason: The body of platyhelminthes is compressed laterally.
3. **Assertion:** Moist skin is present in amphibian.
   Reason: Cutaneous respiration present in amphibians.
4. **Assertion:** All mammals show the characteristics of viviparous.
   Reason: Fertilisation is external in all mammals.
5. **Assertion:** Obelia shows the characteristics of metagenesis; which is equivalent to alternation of generation in plant.
   Reason: In obelia, both polyp and medusa are haploid and diploid in nature.
6. **Assertion:** Ascidia are example of sub - phylum urochordata.
   Reason: In larva stage of urochoradata, notochord is present in tail region.
7. **Assertion:** In bony fishes, fertilisation is usually external.
   Reason: In Claspers are present at pelvic fins of bony fishes.
8. **Assertion:** Pneumatic bones are present in birds.
   Reason: The body weight become reduced during flight
9. **Assertion:** Fat layers are not present in cold blooded animals.
   Reason: Fats are used by cold blooded animals during metabolic process (hibernation).

10. **Assertion:** Cyclostomes can migrate to fresh water for spawning purposes.
    Reason: In marine water, larvae of cyclostomes are metamorphosed.
11. **Assertion:** Sponges are belonging to Porifera group.
    Reason: Canal system is present in sponges.
12. **Assertion:** A shark can stay in water without swimming.
    Reason: Shark has swim bladder; which helps in buoyancy.

***

Chapter-2: Structural organization in animals

- **Introduction**
- **Animal tissue**
- **Cockroach (Insect)**
- **Frog**
- **Golden box**
- **Knowledge points**
- **Multiple Choice Questions (MCQs)**
- **Assertion & Reasons Questions**

INTRODUCTION:

In animal kingdom, both unicellular and multicellular organisms are present. In unicellular organisms, all the physiological actions like digestion, respiration etc. take place within single cell. While in multicellular organisms, different groups of cells work for same functions in organized manner (Hydra is made of different type of cells). Group of similar cells (having specific functions) along with intercellular spaces is called as animal tissue. Four types of tissue present in all complex animals. Organisation of animal tissues gives organs followed by organ systems.

ANIMAL TISSUE:

Animal tissues are categorized into

I. Epithelial tissue
II. Connective tissue
III. Muscular tissue
IV. Neural tissue

(A) Epithelial tissue (epithelium):

Cells of this tissue are compactly arranged with little intercellular matrix and its free surface opens to either outside the environment or body fluids. Both simple (single cell layer) and compound (two or more cell layers) epithelium are two types of epithelial tissues.

Simple epithelial tissue:

Simple epitheliums are divided into squamous, cuboidal and columnar type and present in the lining of body cavities, ducts and tubes; while compound epithelium helps as protection (e.g. body skin).

a) Squamous epithelium:

- i. Present in the wall of blood vessels and air sacs of lungs.
- ii. This epithelium is thin layer of flattened cells with irregular boundaries and helps in diffusions.

b) Cuboidal epithelium:

- i. Present in ducts of glands and tubular part of nephrons of kidney. The PCT of kidney has microvilli.
- ii. This epithelium is thin layer of cube like cells and helps in secretion and absorption.

c) Columnar epithelium:

- i. Present in lining of stomach and intestine
- ii. This epithelium is tall and slender cells having nucleus at its base and helps in secretion and absorption.

Glandular epithelium:
These are specialised columnar or cuboidal epithelial tissues used for secretion.

- ✓ On the basis of number of cells, this epithelium is categorized into unicellular (e.g. Goblet cells of alimentary canal) and multicellular (e.g. Salivary glands) types.
- ✓ On the basis of pouring of their secretion, this epithelium is categorized into exocrine (with ducts or tubes e.g. formation of mucus, saliva, earwax, oil, milk, digestive enzymes and other cell products) and endocrine (without ducts, e.g. formation of hormones) glands.

Compound epithelium:
This type of epithelium is multilayered structure (more than one layer) and protects the body from chemical and mechanical stresses.
e.g.

i. Epidermis or dry surface of skin;
ii. Inner lining or moist surface of buccal cavity, pharynx
iii. Inner lining of salivary and pancreatic ducts

Cell Junctions:
These specialised junctions give both structural and functional link between cells in almost all animal tissue. Three major types of junctions are present in animal tissue i.e. tight (prevent leakage), adhering (keep neighbouring cells together) and gap (rapid transfer of ions, small molecules and sometimes big molecules) junctions respectively.

Connective tissue
These types of tissues are most abundant, widely distributed within the body of complex animals. Connective tissues are linked with other tissue or organs and provide support to the body. These tissues are ranged from soft tissue to specialised tissue (cartilage, bone, adipose and blood).
Cells of this type of tissue (except blood) secrete structural proteins (collagen or elastin) in the form of fibres; which gives elasticity, flexibility and strength to the tissue. Besides this, these cells secrete modified polysaccharides i.e. hyaluronic acid (mucopolysaccharides) in the form of ground substances (matrix); which become accumulated in between cells and fibres. This tissue is categorized into loose, dense and specialised connective tissue.

Loose connective tissue:
Cells and fibres of these tissue (have semi fluid ground substances) are loosely arranged. Areolar tissue is present beneath the skin and contains

fibroblast, macrophages and mast cells. Fibroblasts are fibres producing cells.

Adipose tissue is another type of loose connective tissue; which stores fats. The nutrients which are not utilized immediately converted into fats and store into tissue.

Dense connective tissue:

In this type of tissue, fibroblast and fibres are compactly arranged. On the basis of fibres arrangement pattern, dense tissue is categorized into two types i.e.

- ***Dense regular type***: collagen fibres are in row pattern; e.g. Tendon (connect skeletal muscle to bone); Ligament (connect bone to bone)
- ***Dense irregular type***: fibroblast and fibres are oriented differently. e.g. present in skin.

Specialized connective tissue:

This type of tissue includes cartilages, bones and blood.

a) ***Cartilage:*** This tissue *resists compression* as its intercellular materials is *solid and pliable*. Its cells i.e. chondrocytes produce matrix and enclosed within small cavities along with matrix. In adult, most of the cartilages are converted into bone.
   Examples: outer ear joints, tip of nose, in between vertebrae, forelimbs & hindlimbs of adult etc.
b) ***Bone:*** This tissue provide structural frame to the body and it's inter cellular materials or ground substances are enriched with calcium salts and collagen fibres. So it is *hard and pliable*. Osteocytes (bone cells) present within lacunae. In some bone, bone marrow helps in haemopoiesis. *Examples:* limb bones (weight bearing functions).
c) ***Blood:*** It is a fluid connective tissue and main circulating fluids of our body. It contains plasma and formed elements (RBCs, WBCs & Platelets).

Muscle Tissue:

Muscle is consisting of muscle fibres (long and cylindrical fibres with parallel arrangement). Each muscle fibres are consisting of myofibrils (fine fibrils). Body movements depend upon muscle i.e. the action of muscle fibres (contraction due to stimulation followed by relaxation). There are 3 types of muscle i.e.

1. ***Skeletal muscle:*** This type of muscle is striated and voluntary; which is attached to skeletal bones. e.g. biceps, striate skeletal muscle fire.
2. ***Smooth muscle:*** This type of muscle is fusiform type (taper at both ends), involuntary and not striated. e.g. walls of internal organs (stomach, intestine, blood vessels)
3. ***Cardiac muscle:*** This type of muscle is contractile and involuntary. Here intercalate discs (communication junction) contract as unit.

Neural Tissue:

Body response to changing condition in environment depends upon neural tissue (neurons and neuroglial cells). Neurons (stimulated by external factors, followed by generation electrical disturbance and its transmission through plasma membrane) are excitable cells and units of neural system; while neuroglial cells (> one half volume of neural tissues) support and protect neurons. Adjacent neurons are either stimulate or inhibited after the reaching of electrical disturbance at nerve endings.

Organ and organ system

More than one type of tissues is present in each organ of our body (all four type of tissue present in heart).

Morphology: study of forms or externally visible features.

Anatomy: study of internal features i.e. morphology of internal organs in animals.

COCKROACH (Insect):

Cockroaches (brown or black; bright yellow; red and green; ¼ to 3 inches i.e. 0.6 to 7.6 cm) are belongs to arthropods and can found in tropical regions. They (having long antennae, legs, extended of upper body wall and live in damp places) are nocturnal, omnivorous and act as vectors for several diseases.

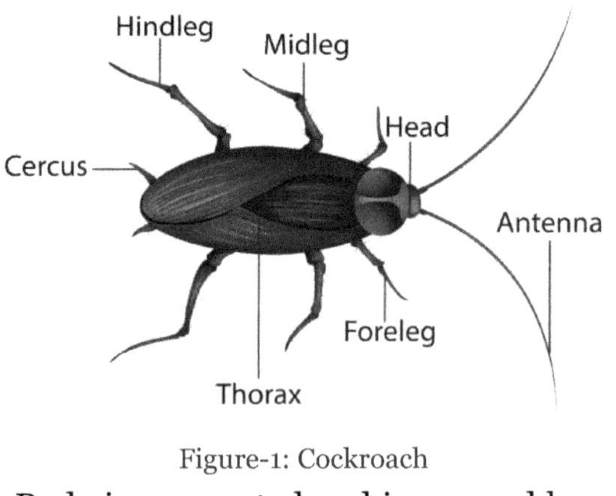

Figure-1: Cockroach

Morphology *(figure-1)*:

Cockroach is about 34-53 mm long. Body is segmented and is covered by brown coloured and hard chitinous exoskeleton; which contains plates called as sclerites (dorsally called as tergites and ventrally called as sternites). These plates are joined together by articular or arthrodial membrane (thin and flexible).

Body of cockroach is divisible into head, thorax and abdomen.

Head

Head is triangular, right angle to body axis and formed by the fusion of six segments. It contains compound eye (1 pairs), antennae (1 pairs, thread like and arises from membranous sockets), mouth parts (used for biting and chewing) and hypo-pharynx (tongue).

a) Sensory receptors are present in antennae and helps in monitoring the environment.
b) Mouth parts are labrum (single, also called upper lip), mandibles (1 pairs), maxillae (1 pairs) and labium (lower lip).

Thorax

It is consisting of 3 parts i.e. prothorax, mesothorax and metathorax. Neck is the short extension part of prothorax, which connect the head. Each part thorax has 1 pair of legs.

a) Mesothorax has 1st pair of wings i.e. forewings/ tegmina (dark, opaque, leathery and cover the hind wing at rest).
b) Metathorax has 2nd pair of wings i.e. hindwings (membranous, transparent and use for flight).

Abdomen

It is consisting of 10 segments in both male and female.

a) In female, 7th sternum (boat shaped) along with 8th and 9th sterna form ***genital pouch/brood***. Spermatheca pore, female gonopore and collateral glands are associates with anterior part of brood.
b) In male, 10th tergum along with 9th tergum and 9th sternum form ***genital pouch/ chamber***. Anus (dorsal), male genital pore (ventral) and gonapophysis are associates with male genital chamber.
c) Anal style (short and thread like) are present in male and absent in female.
d) Anal cerci (jointed filamentous structure; act as sound receptor) are present in both male and female,

Digestive system:

It is the combination of alimentary canal and digestive glands. Alimentary canal is present in body cavity and consisting of foregut (lined with cuticle), mid gut and hindgut (ileum, colon and rectum). In foregut, mouth opens to pharynx (short tubular) followed by oesophagus (narrow tubular), crop (storing of food) and gizzard/proventriculus

a) Gizzard (helps in grinding of food) is consisting of circular muscle (thick and outer layer) and 6 numbers of teeth (chitinous plates; inner and thick).
b) Gastric/ hepatic caeca (6 to 8 blind tubules) present at the junction between foregut and midgut. This caeca secrete ***digestive juice***.
c) Hindgut is comparatively broader than midgut.

Excretory system

Malpighian tubules (100 to 150 numbers; yellow coloured and thin filamentous) are present at the junction in between foregut and midgut.

a) Each tubule is lined with glandular and ciliated cells and absorbs nitrogenous waste products from haemolymph. These nitrogenous waste products are converted into uric acid. So insects are uricotelic organism.
b) Besies this, fat body, urecose gland, nephrocytes, fat body are also helps in excretion

Circulatory System

Circulatory system is consisting of Blood vessels, heart and haemolymph. Blood vessels open to haemocoel; where visceral organs are bathed in haemolymph.

a) Heart (elongated and muscular tube) is present at dorsal side and having funnel shaped chamber (ostia on either side of chamber).
b) Heart pumped blood anteriorly into sinuses.

Respiratory System

This system has trachea; which opens to outside through 10 pairs of spiracles. Tracheoles (thin branching tubes) help in diffusion of gases (oxygen gas) from air to all parts of body. Sphincter regulates the opening of spiracles.

Nervous system

This system is spread throughout the body of cockroach. If the head of cockroach cut off, still the organism lives up to one week. Series of ganglia (fused and segmented form) are present in ventral side and joined by longitudinal connectives. Supra-oesophageal ganglion (brain) supply nerves to antennae and compound eyes.

Sense organs

Antennae, compound eyes (dorsal side of head, 2000 hexagonal ommatidia), maxillary palps, labial palps, anal cerci etc. are the sense organs. Ommatidia helps in mosaic vision (more sensitivity, less resolution and nocturnal vision).

Male Reproductive system

Male reproductive system of cockroach is consisting of testes (1 pairs; in between 4th to 6th abdominal segment), vas deferens (thin), seminal vesicle, ejaculatory duct (opens to male gonopore), mushroom shaped gland (in between 6th and 7th abdominal segment) and external genitalia (male gonapophysis / phallomere).

a) Vas deferens opens to ejaculatory duct through seminal vesicle.
b) In seminal vesicle, sperms are stored and forms bundles called as spermatophores
c) During copulation, spermatophores become discharged.

Female Reproductive system

Ovaries (two in numbers, in between 2nd– 6th abdominal segments), oviducts (two in numbers), vagina, spermatheca (1 pairs; present in 6th segment), genital chamber and ootheca chamber are the components of female reproductive system.

a) Eight numbers of ovarioles are present in each ovary.
b) Vagina is the single median oviduct formed when both oviducts united.
c) Spermatophores (contains sperms) of male cockroach released into spermatheca. Spermatheca opens to genital chamber.

Fertilisation and development

Each ovariole releases one ovum. So 16 ova released at once into genital chamber through oviduct and vagina followed by the release of sperms from spermatheca. It is estimate that 14-16 numbers of ova become fertilized and surrounded by dark reddish to blackish brown colour membrane and formed one ootheca. Female cockroach can hold 9 to 10 numbers of ootheca in its ootheca chamber.

Development of fertilized eggs takes place through nymphal stage (paurometabolous type). Nymph (wings pad present in last nymphal stage) looks like adult but undergo moulting (13 times) and developed into adult (wings present instead of wing pads)

Many species do not have economic importance, while few species entered into human habitat. They are the pest and spread bacterial diseases through contamination of food by their excreta.

FROG:

Figure-2: Frog

Rana tigrina (*figure-2*) belong to class Amphibia and their body temperature varies with surrounding temperature. So they are poikilotherms (cold blooded animals). Besides this, they show the characteristics of camouflage (change in colour to hide from their enemies) and this protective colouration is called mimicry. Again, this animals go for aestivation (summer sleep) and hibernation.(winter sleep).

Skin: smooth and slippery (due to mucus), olive green with dark irregular spot (dorsal site), pale yellow (ventral side), absorb water through skin (never drink).

Body:

Body is consisting of head and trunk (neck and tail absent). Eyes are covered by nictitating membrane. Ears/ membranous tympanum are present on either side of eyes and receive sound signal.

Limb helps in walking, leaping, burrowing, swimming; 5 digits in forelimbs and 4 digits in hind limbs; webbed digits in feet. Copulatory pad is present in male frog.

Digestive system (alimentary canal + digestive glands)

a) Alimentary canal of frog is short (because they are carnivorous). It is consisting of mouth, buccal cavity (having bilobed tongue), pharynx, oesophagus (short tube), stomach (release HCl and gastric juice), intestine (final digestion takes place), rectum (having undigested solid waste) and cloaca.
b) Bile is secreted from liver, stored in gall bladder and released into duodenum through common bile duct. Bile helps in emulsification of fats.
c) Pancreatic juice (contains digestive enzymes) secreted from pancreas and released into duodenum through common bile duct. This juice helps in digestion of carbohydrates and proteins.
d) Chyme is the partially digested food which is passed from stomach to duodenum.
e) Vlli and microvilli of intestine helps in absorption of digested food. Undigested food passés through cloaca.

Respiratory system

Respiration in frog takes place in water (through skin i.e. cutaneous respiration) and in land (through buccal cavity, skin and lungs).

I. One pair lungs (sac like, pink colour and elongated) are present at upper part of thorax or trunk region and respiration through lungs is called pulmonary respiration. The respiratory passage is nostrils, buccal cavity and lungs.

II. Gaseous exchange takes place through skin during aestivation and hibernation.

Blood vascular and lymphatic system

Frog shows closed type circulatory system. Blood vascular system is consisting of heart, blood vessels and blood.

a) ***Heart*** *(present at upper part of body cavity)* is muscular structure and three chambered i.e. atria (2) and ventricle (1). Here sinus venosus (triangular and join right atrium) receives blood from vena cava and ventricle opens to conus arteriosus (sac like, present at ventral side of heart),
b) ***Blood vessels*** are arterial system (carry blood from heart to all body parts), venous system (collect blood from different part of body to heart), hepatic portal system (here portal vein connect to liver from intestine) and renal portal system (portal vein connect to kidney).
c) ***Blood*** *(plasma+ cells)***:** During circulation, blood carries nutrients, water and gases. Blood cells are consisting of RBCs (nucleated, contains haemoglobin), WBCs and platelets.

The lymphatic system is consisting of lymph, lymph nodes and lymph channels. Lymph don't have RBCs and certain proteins.

Excretory system

Excretory system is consisting of a pair of kidneys (dark red, compact and bean shaped), ureters, cloaca and urinary bladder is the component of excretory system.

a) Kidneys are present posteriorly on both side of vertebral column and contain several uriniferous tubules (nephrons).
b) Ureters are two in numbers and act as urinogenital duct in male; while in female both ureter and oviduct open separately.
c) Urinary bladder (thin walled) present at ventral side of rectum and opens into cloaca.

Here urea is the nitrogenous waste products.

Control and coordination

Both neural system and endocrine glands are the components of control and coordination of frog.

Nervous system

It is consisting of CNS (Brain and spinal cord), PNS (cranial and spinal nerves) and ANS (sympathetic and parasympathetic).

a) Brain of frog is present in brain box/cranium (bony structure); which is consisting of forebrain (olfactory lobes+ paired cerebral hemisphere+ unpaired diencephalon), mid brain (paired optic lobes) and hind brain (cerebellum and medulla oblongata).

b) Medulla oblongata connects to spinal cord through foramen of magnum. Ten pairs of cranial nerves are arises from brain.

Endocrine glands secrete hormones; which helps in chemical coordination in the body. Pituitary, pineal body, thyroid, parathyroid, thymus, pancreas (islets of langerhans), adrenals and gonads are the major endocrine glands.

Sense organs

Sensory papillae (touch), taste buds (taste), nasal epithelium (smell), eyes (vision), tympanum with internal ears (hearing) are the sense organs of frog. Out of these sense organs, eyes and internal ears are well organised; while remaining are cellular aggregations.

- Eyes (1 pairs) are simple type (one unit), spherical and present in orbit of skull.
- External ear is absent. Tympanum with internal ears helps in both hearing and balancing (equilibrium).

Reproductive system

a) The male reproductive syste of frog is consisting of testes (1 pairs, yellowish and ovoid), vasa efferentia (10 to 12 numbers), Bidders canal, urinogenital duct (arises from kidney and connect to cloaca) and cloaca.

  - Testes adhere to kidney by structure called as mesorchium (double old peritoneum).
  - Cloaca is small and helps in passage for faecal matter, urine and sperms.

b) Female reproductive system of frog is consisting of ovaries (1 pairs, nearer to kidney but not connected), oviducts (1 pairs) and cloaca. Around 2500 to 3000 ova are produced at a time.

c) Fertilisation (external, in water medium); development (indirect, through tadpole larva); this larva undergo metamorphosis.

GOLDEN BOX-1

Explain the function of ureter in frog?

In male frog, ureters are also called as urinogenital duct. This duct helps in both passage of urine(excretion) and passage of sperm (reproduction) from kidney to cloaca. In female frog, ureters help in passage of urine from kidney to cloaca.

Importance

i. Frog protect crop by eating insects.
ii. Maintain ecological balance (part of food chain and food web)

iii. In some countries, le of fro is use as food)

DIFFERENCE BETWEEN:

Epithelial tissue	Connective tissue
1. In this tissue, cells are tightly packed with negligible inter cellular space.	1. Here cells are separated by abundant extra cellular matrix.
2. These tissues are generally avascular.	2. These tissues are mostly vascular.
3. Basement membrane is present'.	3. Basement membrane is usually absent.
4. This tissue helps in protection, absorption, secretion, excretion etc.	4. This tissue helps in support, protection, binding, storage etc.

KNOWLEDGE POINTS:

- ***Basement membrane*** is consisting of two layers i.e. basal lamina (consisting of proteins like laminin and collagen along with glycoprotein and proteoglycan) and reticular lamina (consisting of collagen proteins). Epithelial tissue produces basal lamina, while connective tissue produces reticular lamina. Epithelial tissue is avascular and depends upon adjacent connective tissue.
- Covering and lining epithelium (surface epithelium) and glandular epithelium are two types of epithelial tissue.
- Stratified squamous epithelium can be keratinized or non-keratinized. ***Keratin*** (intracellular protein) protects underlying tissue from heat, microbes and chemicals. Cells considered dead when the level of keratin increases in cells.
- The examination of epithelial cells can be done through ***Papanicolaou test.***
- There are two types of glands i.e. Exocrine (with ducts, its secretion may contain enzymes) and Endocrine (without duct, release hormones).
- ***Ground substances*** are consisting of large organic molecules (combination of polysaccharides and proteins) and water. Hyaluronic acids, chondritin sulfate, dermatan sulfate and

keratin sulfate are the polysaccharides or glycoaminoglycans (GAGs). Proteoglycans are formed due to combination of these polysaccharides (except hyaluronic acid) with proteins. Hyaluronic acids helps in binding of cells together, lubricate joints etc. Hyaluronidase is the enzyme produced by sperm cell, WBCs and some bacteria.

- ***Liposuction*** is a surgical procedure in which small amount of adipose tissue is suck out from areas of body. In ***cryolipolysis (Coolsculpting)***, fat cells become killed by cold temperature treatment because fat crystallizes faster.

MULTIPLE CHOICE QUESTIONS (MCQ)-1:

1. In connective tissue sheaths, this is the correct sequence stretching from the outermost to the innermost layer
   (a) perineurium, epineurium, endoneurium
   (b) epineurium, endoneurium, perineurium
   (c) perineurium, endoneurium, epineurium
   (d) epineurium, perineurium, endoneurium
2. This is the difference between a nerve and a neuron
   (a) nerves are made of grey matter while neurons of white matter
   (b) consists of different number of cells
   (c) one has motor and other has sensory function
   (d) nerves are present in central nervous system only
3. The only connective tissue without fibroblasts is
   (a) Cartilage
   (b) Areolar tissue
   (c) Bone
   (d) Blood
4. In which tissue cells, Lacunae are enclosed
   (a) Bone tissue
   (b) Cartilage
   (c) Both(a) and (b)
   (d) muscular tissue
5. Mast cells are linked to
   (a) Neural tissue
   (b) Endocrine glands
   (c) Exocrine glands
   (d) Areolar connective tissue
6. Categorization of epithelial tissue is based on this
   (a) Type of matrix

(b) Function
(c) Structural modification
(d) Non voluntary or voluntary action

7. Which is correct about epithelial tissue?
(a) Lack of intercellular matrix
(b) Lack of nerve supply
(c) Lack of blood supply
(d) Lack of free surface

8. Function of gap junction is to
(a) Stop substance from leaking across a tissue
(b) Facilitate communication between adjoining cells by connecting cytoplasm for rapid transfer of ions, small molecules and some large molecules
(c) Separate two cells from each other
(d) Performing cementing to keep neighboring cells together

9. Pick the correctly matched pair
(a) Areolar tissue – loose connective tissue
(b) Cartilage – loose connective tissue
(c) Adipose tissue – dense connective tissue
(d) Tendon – specialized connective tissue

10. In which of the following preparations are you likely to come across cell junctions most frequently?
(a) Ciliated epithelium
(b) Hyaline cartilage
(c) Thrombocytes
(d) Tendon

MULTIPLE CHOICE QUESTIONS (MCQ)-2:

1. Which type of tissue correctly matches with its location?
(a) Areolar tissue & Tendons
(b) Smooth muscle & Wall of intestine
(c) Transitional epithelium & Tip of nose
(d) Cuboidal epithelium & lining of stomach

2. Smooth muscles are
(a) Voluntary, multinucleate, cylindrical
(b) Voluntary, spindle-shaped, uninucleate
(c) Involuntary, cylindrical, striated
(d) Involuntary, fusiform, non-straited

3. Choose the correctly matched pair:

(a) Adipose tissue – Dense connective tissue
(b) Tendon – Specialized connective tissue
(c) Areolar tissue – Loose connective tissue
(d) Cartilage – Loose connective tissue

4. Choose the correctly matched pair:
(a) Moist surface of buccal cavity – Glandular epithelium
(b) Tubular parts of nephrons – Cuboidal epithelium
(c) Inner surface of bronchioles – Squamous epithelium
(d) Inner lining of salivary ducts – Ciliated epithelium

5. The ciliated columnar epithelial cells in humans are known to occur in
(a) Fallopian tubes and urethra
(b) Bronchioles and fallopian tubes
(c) Bile duct and oesophagus
(d) Eustachian tube and stomach lining

6. Which of the following are correctly states as it happen in the common cockroach?
(a) The food is ground by mandibles and gizzard.
(b) Oxygen is transported by haemoglobin in blood.
(c) The nitrogenous excretory product is urea.
(d) Malpighian tubules are excretory organs projecting out from the colon.

7. The supportive skeletal structures in the human external ears and in the nose tip are examples of
(a) Cartilage
(b) Areolar tissue
(c) Bone
(d) Ligament

8. In which tissue, the fibres and fibroblasts are completely packed?

(a) Dense irregular connective tissue
(b) Dense regular connective tissue
(c) Both (a) and (b)
(d) Cartilage

9. Which structures are joined by tendons?
(a) Skeletal muscles to ligaments
(b) Skeletal muscles to bones
(c) Both (a) and (b)
(d) Bones to ligaments

10. Which of the following tissue is not present in skin?

(a) Aerolar tissue
(b) Epithelial tissue
(c) Dense connective
(d) All of these

11. Which of the following is/are example of dense connective tissue?
(a) Ligament
(b) Tendon
(c) Cartilage
(d) All of these

12. Which portion of cartilage provides it with solidity, pliability and resistance to compression?
(a) Collagen fibres
(b) Calcium content
(c) Chondrocytes
(d) Intracellular material

13. In male cockroaches, sperms are stored in which part of the reproductive system?
(a) Seminal vesicles
(b) Mushroom glands
(c) Testes
(d) Vas deferens

14. Select the correct statement from the ones given below with respect to *Periplaneta americana*.
(a) Males bear a pair of short thread like anal styles.
(b) Nervous system is located dorsally, it consists of segmentally arranged ganglia joined by a pair of longitudinal connectives.
(c) There are 16 very long Malpighian tubules present at the junctions of midgut and hindgut.
(d) Grinding of foods is carried out only by the mouth parts.

15. What external changes are visible after the last moult of a cockroach nymph?
(a) Mandibles become harder
(b) Anal cerci develops
(c) Both forewings and hind wings develop
(d) Labium develops

16. How many oothecae is produced by female cockroach?
(a) 9 to 10
(b) 14 to 16

(c) 13
(d) 1 to 2

17. The nymph of cockroach is grown by moulting for about ________ times to reach the adult form.
(a) 10
(b) 12
(c) 11
(d) 13

18. Which one of the following is incorrect statement about cockroach?
(a) Development in *Periplanta americana* is paurometabolus type.
(b) They are pest because they destroy food and contaminate it with their smelly excreta.
(c) All species have economic importance.
(d) Next to last nymphal stage have wing pads.

19. Which one of the following is the correct statement about cockroach?
(a) Each eye consists of about 1000 hexagonal ommatidia.
(b) Anal style is present only in male cockroach.
(c) Anal cerci are present only in female cockroach.
(d) Each oothecae contain 12 to 14 eggs.

20. How many ganglia lies in thorax and in the abdomen of cockroach?
(a) 1 and 2
(b) 3 and 6
(c) 6 and 3
(d) 2 and 1

21. If the head of cockroach is cut off, it will live for as long as
(a) 4 weeks
(b) 2 weeks
(c) 1 week
(d) 3 weeks

22. Mosaic vision means
(a) Less sensitivity and less resolution
(b) Less sensitivity and more resolution
(c) More sensitivity and less resolution
(d) More sensitivity and more resolution

23. A pair of testes in cockroach lies in
(a) 6 to 8 abdominal segment
(b) 2 to 4 abdominal segment
(c) 4 to 6 abdominal segment
(d) 4 to 7 abdominal segment

24. External genitalia in cockroach is represented by
    (a) Phallomere
    (b) Male gonophysis
    (c) Both (a) and (b).
    (d) Ejaculatory duct
25. Compared to those of humans, the erythrocytes in frog are
    (a) Without nucleus but with haemoglobin
    (b) Nucleated and with haemoglobin
    (c) Nucleated and without haemoglobin
    (d) Very much smaller and fewer

MULTIPLE CHOICE QUESTIONS (MCQ)-3:

1. This feature is not found in *Periplaneta americana*
    (a) Schizocoelom as the body cavity
    (b) Metamerically segmented body
    (c) Indeterminate and radial cleavage during embryonic development
    (d) Exoskeleton composed of N-acetylglucose-amine
2. Sperms in male cockroaches are stored in which part of the reproductive system?
    (a) Vas Deferens
    (b) Testes
    (c) Mushroom glands
    (d) Seminal vesicles
3. What are the regions of the body of the cockroach?
    (a) Head, Thorax, Abdomen
    (b) Head,Thorax
    (c) Head, Abdomen
    (d) Head, Body, Tail
4. What material is the exoskeleton of the cockroach made of?
    (a) Calcium
    (b) Chitin
    (c) Collagen
    (d) Cellulose
5. The cockroach body is covered by an exoskeleton made of ______.
    (a) Pronotum
    (b) Tegmina
    (c) Sclerites
    (d) labrum
6. What is the membrane that joins tergites and sternites in cockroach?
    (a) Vesicular membrane
    (b) Capillary membrane

(c) Arthrodial membrane
(d) Arthropodal membrane

7. The fusion of how many segments makes up the head part of cockroach?
(a) 4
(b) 5
(c) 2
(d) 6

8. Which of these is true about antennae of cockroaches?
(a) They arise from membranous sockets
(b) They are present in the thorax region
(c) They have 2 pairs
(d) They lack sensory receptors

9. Which of these structures act as the tongue of the cockroach?
(a) Maxilla
(b) Labium
(c) Labrum
(d) Hypopharynx

10. How many legs are there in each thoracic segment of a cockroach?
(a) One
(b) Two
(c) Four
(d) Six

11. The first pair of wings of cockroach arises from ________.
(a) Abdomen
(b) Prothorax
(c) Mesothorax
(d) Metathorax

ASSERTION AND REASON QUESTIONS: *Read the* **assertion** *and* **reason** *carefully to mark the correct option out of the options given below:*

(a) If both the assertion and the reason are true and the reason is a correct explanation of the assertion.
(b) If both the assertion and reason are true but the reason is not a correct explanation of the assertion.
(c) If the assertion is true but the reason is false.
(d) If both the assertion and reason are false.

1. **Assertion:** For human beings, cockroaches are harmful.

Reason: Several diseases are easily transmitted through cockroach.

2. **Assertion:** Cockroach can live up to one week after its head become cut off.
   Reason: The head of cockroach contains a bit of a nervous system.
3. **Assertion:** Both hibernation and aestivation characters are present in Frogs.
   Reason: So frog protects themselves from extreme heat and cold conditions respectively.
4. **Assertion:** Frogs are cold blooded animals.
   Reason: The body temperature of frog varies according to change in environmental temperature.
5. **Assertion:** Sexual dimorphism is the characteristic features of frog.
   Reason: Vocal sac present in male frog only.
6. **Assertion:** Ecological balance can also be maintained by frog.
   Reason: In between flood web and food chain of ecosystem, frog can be considered as the important link.
7. **Assertion:** Muscle fibres are contractile in nature.
   Reason: Muscle tissues can shorten forcefully and can return back to relaxed state.
8. **Assertion:** In animals, cells are communicated with each other through gap junctions.
   Reason: In gap junction, cytoplasms of adjacent cells are connected.
9. **Assertion:** Smooth muscle fibres are striated.
   Reason: In skeletal muscle fibre, both thick and thin filaments are arranged in both regular and alternate ways.
10. **Assertion:** Unstriated muscles are voluntary in nature.
    Reason: According to will, unstriated muscles can be moved.
11. **Assertion:** In cardiac muscle, intercalated discs are the important regions.
    Reason: Intercalated discs are the junctions, through which communication of muscle contraction waves takes place.
12. **Assertion:** Both underlying and overlying tissue are protected by epithelial tissues.
    Reason: Exchange of materials takes place across the surfaces of epithelial tissues.

Chapter-3: Breathing and Exchange of Gases

- **Introduction**
- **Human respiratory system**
- **Mechanism of breathing**
- **Respiratory volume and capacity**
- **Physiology of respiration**
- **Regulation of respiration**
- **Disorders of respiratory system**
- **Golden box**
- **Knowledge points**
- **Multiple choice questions (MCQs)**
- **Assertion & Reason questions**

INTRODUCTION:

Animals have different categories of breathings (Based on habitats and level of organization).

1. Simple diffusion through body surface (sponges, coelenterates, flatworms, etc.)
2. Moist cuticle (Earthworms)
3. Tracheal tubes (Insects)
4. Gills (moist aquatic arthropods and mollusks, fishes; branchial respiration)
5. Lungs or vascularised bags (terrestrial forms I.e. amphibians, reptiles, birds and mammals; pulmonary respiration)
6. Moist skin (frogs; cutaneous respiration)

HUMAN RESPIRATORY SYSTEM *(figure-1)*:

- External nostrils (above upper lips),
- Nasal chamber,
- Pharynx (common passage for food an air),
- Larynx (cartilaginous box; sound box),
- Trachea,
- Bronchi (primary, secondary and tertiary),
- Bronchioles (initial, terminal),
- Alveoli,
- Lungs (having bronchi, bronchioles and alveoli; two numbers; covered by a double layer pleural membranes; friction on lungs surface is reduced by pleural fluid)

Thoracic chamber: vertebral column (Dorsal side), Sternum (Ventral side), Ribs (lateral sides), Diaphragm (lower side; dome shaped)

Respiration involves

a) Atmospheric air enter and CO_2 released out from alveoli of lungs (pulmonary ventilation or Breathing)
b) In alveolar membrane, exchange of O_2 and CO_2 gases by diffusion.
c) Gases are transported through blood.
d) In between blood and tissues, exchange of O_2 and CO_2 gases by diffusion method.
e) O_2 gases become utilized within cells and released CO_2 gases due to cellular respiration.

MECHANISM OF BREATHING:

Inspiration: Contraction of diaphragm and external inter-costal muscles (thoracic volume increases); Intra-pulmonary pressure < atmospheric pressure (- ve pressure in lungs); Atmospheric air enter into lungs.

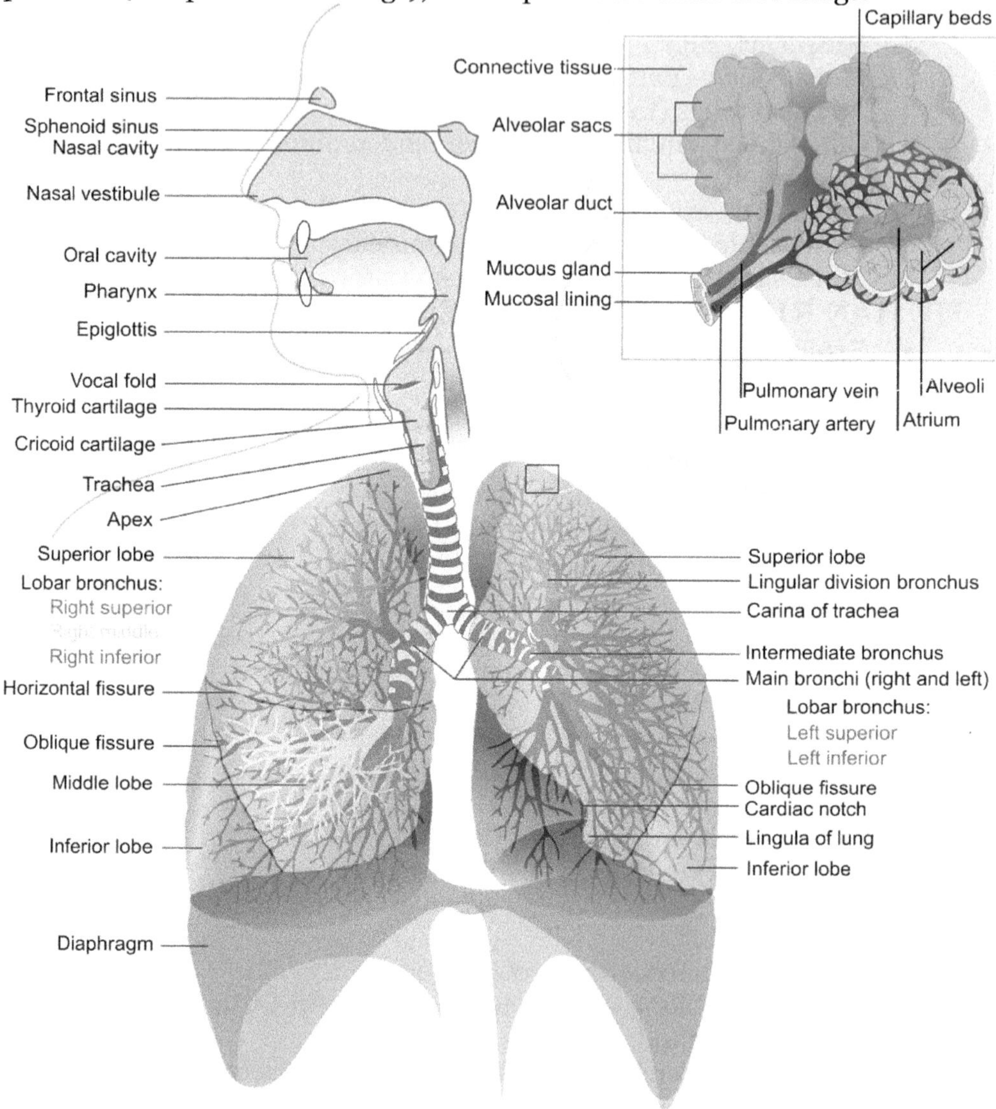

Figure-1: Human respiratory system

Expiration: Relaxation of diaphragm and external inter-costal muscles (thoracic volume decreases); Intra-pulmonary pressure > atmospheric pressure (+ve pressure in lungs) ; Alveolar air is released out.

- Inspiration and expiration strength can be increased with the help of abdominal muscles.
- Breathing rate in healthy man: 12-16 times /min.
- Spiro meter: estimate breathing movements

RESPIRATORY VOLUMES AND CAPACITIES *(figure-4)*:

1) **Tidal Volume** (TV, 500mL): The amount of air taken or expelled out from lungs during a normal respiration.
2) **Inspiratory Reserve Volume** (IRV, 2500 mL to 3000 mL): Extra amount of air taken into the lungs during a forcible inspiration.
3) **Expiratory Reserve Volume** (ERV, 1000mL to 1100 mL): Extra amount of air expelled out from lungs during a forcible inspiration.
4) **Residual Volume** (RV, 1100 mL to 1200 mL): The amount of air remains within lungs after a forcible expiration. Can be used in clinical significance.
5) **Inspiratory Capacity** (IC= TV+IRV): Amount of air taken into the lungs after a normal expiration.
6) **Expiratory Capacity** (EC= TV+ERV): Amount of air expelled out from lungs after a normal inspiration.
7) **Functional Residual Capacity** (FRC= ERV+RV): The amount of air will remain in the lungs after a normal expiration.

PHYSIOLOGY OF RESPIRATION:

Exchange of gases *(figure2)*:

Exchange of gases (by simple diffusion mechanism) takes place at two places i.e. in alveoli and in blood and tissues.

Factors responsible for simple diffusion are

a) Partial pressure of O_2 and CO_2 gases
b) Solubility of gases (CO_2 have 20-25 times solubility than O_2 gases)

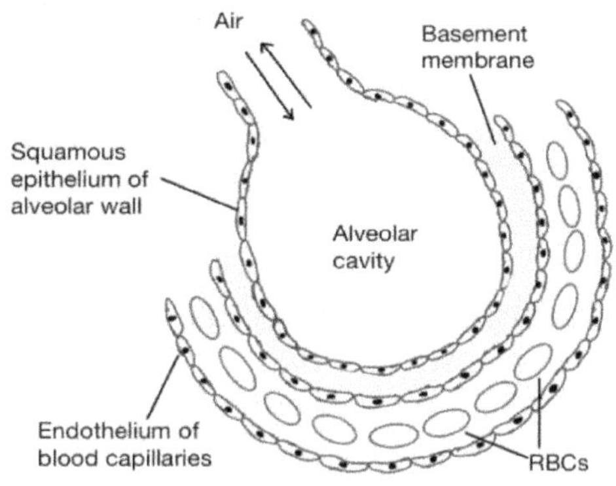

Figure-2: Exchange of gases in alveoli of lungs

c) Thickness of membrane (much less than a millimeter)

Diffusion membrane= Squamous epithelium of alveoli (thin)+ Endothelium of alveolar capillaries + Basement substance (basement membrane of squamous epithelium and endothelium respectively).

GOLDEN BOX-1:

What is vital capacity? Explain its significance?

The volume of air expelled out from lungs after forceful inspiration is called as vital capacity (VC). It is the sum of tidal volume (TV) and inspiratory reserve volume (IRV).

The significances of vital capacity are

a. Vital capacity determines the strength and capacity of respiratory muscle and lungs.
b. Respiratory health conditions (like asthma, neuromuscular disorders etc.) can be determined by Vital capacity.
c. Higher vital capacity in athletes represents better aerobic fitness

The volume of air remains within the lungs after a normal breathing is called_____?

The volume of air remains within the lungs after normal expiration or tidal volume or normal breathing is called as functional residual capacity (FRC). It is the combination of Residual volume (RV) and Expiratory reserve volume (ERV). The value of FRC may vary on the basis of age, body size and sex.FRC= ERV (1000 to 1100 ml) + RV (1100 to 1200 ml) = 2100 to 2300 ml

Diffusion of gases occurs only in the alveolar region of lungs. Explain it?

Diffusion of gases takes place in alveolar regions only but not in other parts of respiratory system because. Alveoli provide large surface area for diffusion of gases and surrounded by dense networks of capillaries. Again inner surface of alveoli is moist, that dissolve gasses before diffusion across diffusion membrane. Besides this, alveoli are lined with simple squamous epithelial tissue and are the component of thin diffusion membrane (thickness < 1mm). Other structures do not have such characteristics.

Transport of Oxygen

Oxygen gases (around 97% by RBCs and 3% by plasma in dissolved state) are transported through blood medium. Haemoglobin pigment present in RBCs and bind with O_2 and form oxyhaemoglobin (reversible manner). Four molecules of O_2 (maximum) can be carried by one haemoglobin molecule.

The binding capacity of O2 gas with haemoglobin depends upon following factors

1. partial pressure of O2
2. Partial pressure of CO2
3. hydrogen ion concentration
4. temperature

Oxygen dissociation curve (sigmoid curve) determines the percentage of haemoglobin saturation with O2 against partial pressure of O2 and useful to study the effect of pCO2, H+ concentration, etc., on binding capability of O2 with haemoglobin.

- Favorable conditions for oxyhaemolobin formation in alveoli site are greater pO2, lesser pCO2, low H+ concentration and less temperature.
- Favorable conditions for oxyhaemolobin formation in tissue site are lesser pO2, greater pCO2, high H+ concentration and high temperature.

In normal physiological condition, 100 ml of oxygenated blood provide 5ml of O2 to tissue.

Transport of Carbon dioxide

Carbon dioxide gases (around 20-25% by RBCs, 70% as bicarbonate and 7% through plasma in a dissolved state) are transported through blood medium *(figure-3)*.

CO2+ haemoglobin = carbamino-haemoglobin

- ✓ Condition for carbamino-haemoglobin formation: High pCO2 and low pO2 in tissue.
- ✓ Condition for CO2 dissociation from carbamino-haemoglobin: High pO2 and low pCO2 in alveoli.

Carbonic anhydrase (C A) = Enzymes which is abundant within RBCs and less quantities in plasma. This enzyme is involved in following reactions. Increase in the level CO2 in tissue leads to the formation of HCO_3^- and H+ in blood. The level of CO2 in alveoli leads to formation CO2 and H2O from bicarbonate (HCO_3^-). Approx. 4ml of CO2 delivered in alveoli from 100ml of deoxygenated blood *(figure-4)*.

GOLDEN BOX-2:

Explain the transport mechanisms for CO2?

Carbon dioxide (CO_2) is transported in the blood from body tissues to the lungs through three major mechanisms. These mechanisms allow CO_2 to be effectively carried despite its relatively low solubility in plasma. Here's a breakdown:The transportation of CO_2 takes place through three mechanisms i.e. (1) around 7% are in dissolved state, (2) around 20 to 25% are in carbaminohaemoglobin and (3) 70% as bicarbonate.

Find out pO_2 and pCO_2 in the atmospheric air as compared to in the alveolar air?

pO_2 higher, pCO_2 lesser

Explain inspiration at normal conditions?

During Inspiration, contraction of both EICM (external inter coastal muscle) and diaphragm takes place. That leads to increase in thoracic cavity followed by increase in lungs volume. Then lungs pressure decreases. That leads to inflow of air into lungs. So inspiration is an active process.

Explain the regulation of respiration?

Respiration is regulated by both neural control and chemical feedback. Both DRG (dorsal respiratory group) and VRG (ventral respiratory group) are present in medulla oblongata, while pneumotaxic centre is present in pons varolii. DRG is connected with EICM and diaphragm and involved in normal breathing, while VRG is connected with EICM, IICM, diaphragm and abdominal muscle and involved in forceful breathing. Pneumotaxic centre is inhibitory in function and helps in expiration.

Chemosensitive area is also present in medulla oblongata and sensitive to CO_2 and H^+ ion concentration in our body. Again chemoreceptors are present in aortic arc and carotid artery. These receptors are also sensitive to CO_2 and H^+ ion concentration in our body. In this way, the breathing rate becomes increased. During sleep, exercise, stress, the respiration rate is also changed.

Effect of pCO_2 on oxygen transport.

According to Bohr's effect, Increase in pCO_2 and H^+ ion concentration causes shifting of oxygen haemoglobin dissociation curve towards right. That means increased pCO_2 level decreases the hemoglobin's affinity for oxygen.

REGULATION OF RESPIRATION:

The respiratory rhythm is maintained and moderated by neural system. Neural centers are present in medulla oblongata (respiratory rhythm centre; causing regulation of respiration) and pons varoli region (pneumotaxic centre; decrease inspiration and alter respiratory rate) of brain.

- Chemosensitive area: present nearer to respiratory rhythm centre; Highly sensitive to CO2 and H+
- Chemo receptors in aortic arch and carotid artery: recognize changes in CO2 and H+ concentration.
- Role of O2 gases is insignificant in regulation of respiration.

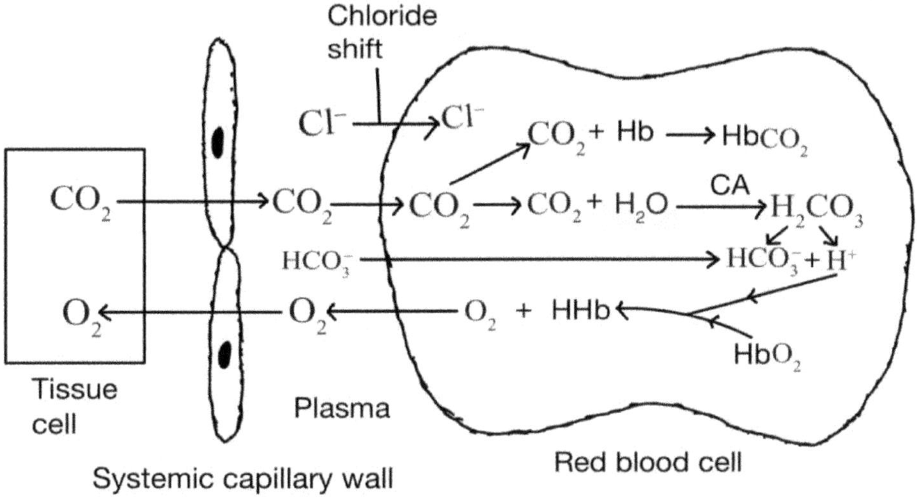

Figure-3: Transportation of gases from body tissue

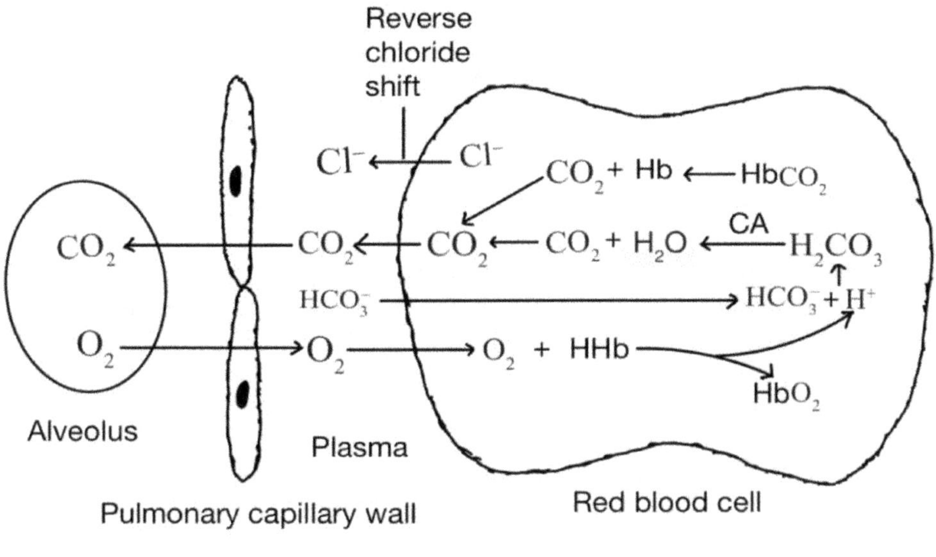

Figure-4: Transportation of gases from alveoli of lungs

GOLDEN BOX-3:

Explain the respiratory process in a man at high altitude?

When altitude increases, the atmospheric pressure becomes decreased. That means the partial pressure of the oxygen is also decreased. So the entry of oxygen into blood through diffusion process becomes harder. Then respiratory rate and heart rate of the person become increased. Besides this, person may feel tiredness or weakness.

At high altitude, if the person stay for days to weeks. Then the level of RBCs production becomes increased along with efficient uses of oxygen at cellular level. Besides this, capillary density is also increased in muscles.

Explain the exchange of gases in an insect?

Spiracles → Tracheae → Tracheoles → Cells

Explain oxygen dissociation curve and give any reason for its sigmoidal pattern?

The oxygen dissociation curve is sigmoid or S- shaped due to cooperative binding of oxygen with haemoglobin. There are four subunits in haemoglobin and each subunit bind with one oxygen molecule. The binding of first oxygen with haemoglobin causes conformational changes in hemoglobin. Then it is easier for the binding of next oxygen molecules and increases the affinity of haemoglobin for oxygen.

At low pO_2, the affinity of haemoglobin for oxygen is also low. When pO_2 increases, then the affinity become rapidly increases and leads to steep rise. Then haemoglobin becomes nearly saturated at high oxygen level. Later the curve becomes flattened.

Q. Define Tidal volume? Find out its value in a healthy human in an hour.

A. The deficiency of oxygen in body tissues at normal blood flow into that region is called hypoxia. The hypoxia condition can be created at high altitude, lungs diseases, anemia, choking, CO poisoning etc. The symptoms of hypoxia are rapid breathing, breath shortness, headache, dizziness etc. Treatments include oxygen therapy and CPR (cardiopulmonary resuscitation) in emergency conditions.

DISORDERS OF RESPIRATORY SYSTEM:

- ✓ **Asthma**: Inflammation of bronchi and bronchioles leads to wheezing (difficulty in breathing)

- ✓ **Emphysema**: Cigarette smoking is the major factor for alveolar damages and causing decrease in respiratory surface area.
- ✓ **Occupational Respiratory Disorders**: Long exposure to dust in industry can cause inflammation among peoples and can leads to fibrosis (proliferation of fibrous tissues) and serious lung damages.

DIFFERENCE BETWEEN:

IRV	ERV
1. Inspiratory Reserve Volume 2. The volume of air taken into the lungs forcefully over tidal volume. 3. 2500-3000 ml per breath	1. Expiratory Reserve Volume 2. The volume of air expelled out from lungs forcefully over tidal volume. 3. 1000-1100 ml per breath
IC	**EC**
1. Inspiratory Capacity 2. The volume of air taken into the lungs forcefully after normal expiration. 3. 3000-3500 ml per breath 4. TV+ IRV	1. Expiratory Capacity 2. The volume of air expelled out from lungs forcefully after normal inspiration. 3. 1600-1700 ml per breath 4. TV+ERV
VC	**TLC**
1. Vital Capacity 2. The volume of air exhaled from lungs forcefully after maximum inhalation. 3. 4000-4600 ml per breath 4. TV+ IRV+ ERV	1. Total lungs Capacity 2. The volume of air present in lungs after maximum inhalation. 3. 6000 ml per breath 4. TV+ERV+ IRV+ RV

KNOWLEDGE POINTS:

- ❖ ***Otorhinolaryngology*** is the diagnosis and treatment of diseases in ears, nose and throat (ENT). The shape of external nose can be altered by procedure called as Rhinoplasty.
- ❖ ***Tonsilities*** is the inflammation of tonsils and can obstruct breathing during sleeping. If it appears frequently, then it should be surgically removed out and the procedure is called as

Tonsillectomy.

- The inflammation of larynx can be takes place due to smoking of cigarette and called as ***laryngitis***. It can leads to cancer of larynx.
- In ***pneumothorax***, air present in pleural cavities. If problem is small, then it will resolved by its own. In complex situation, chest tube should be introduced for its evacuation. If blood or pus is present in pleural cavities, then it is called as ***hemothorax***.
- If alveoli donot open due to lack of surfactant is called as ***respiratory distress syndrome (RDS).***
- If the level of PCO2 slightly increases from 40mmng is called ***hypercapnia***.
- ***Hypoxia*** is the condition at which there is deficiency O2 level in tissue. This condition occur due to (a) low Po2 in arterial blood (hypoxic hypoxia), (b) little functioning of haemoglobin (anemic hypoxia), (c) reduce blood flow to tissue (ischemic hypoxia), (d) when tissue unable to use O2 (histotoxic hypoxia).

MULTIPLE CHOICE QUESTIONS (MCQ)-1:

1. During inhalation, which muscle contracts to increase the volume of the thoracic cavity?
   (a) Pectoral muscles
   (b) Diaphragm
   (c) Intercostal muscles
   (d) Abdominal muscles
2. Which of the following respiratory disorders is characterized by chronic inflammation and narrowing of the airways?
   (a) Emphysema
   (b) Pneumonia
   (c) Tuberculosis
   (d) Asthma
3. What is the role of surfactant in the alveoli of the lungs?
   (a) It transports oxygen in the blood.
   (b) It reduces surface tension, preventing alveolar collapse.
   (c) It promotes carbon dioxide diffusion.
   (d) It facilitates mucus production.
4. In which form is most of the carbon dioxide transported in the blood?

(a) As free gas molecules
(b) Dissolved in plasma
(c) Bound to haemoglobin
(d) As bicarbonate ions

5. Which part of the respiratory system is responsible for exchanging gases with the bloodstream?
(a) Larynx
(b) Trachea
(c) Bronchi
(d) Alveoli

6. What is the term for the volume of air that can be forcefully exhaled after a normal exhalation?
(a) Vital capacity
(b) Inspiratory reserve volume
(c) Expiratory reserve volume
(d) Residual volume

7. Which part of the brainstem is responsible for regulating breathing?
(a) Pons
(b) Cerebellum
(c) Medulla oblongata
(d) None of the above

8. What is the term for the maximum amount of air that can be exhaled after a maximum inhalation?
(a) Residual volume
(b) Vital capacity
(c) Inspiratory reserve volume
(d) Expiratory reserve volume

9. Which part of the brain regulates the rate and depth of breathing?
(a) Cerebrum
(b) Cerebellum
(c) Medulla oblongata
(d) Hypothalamus

10. Which gas is released as a byproduct of anaerobic respiration in muscles during strenuous exercise?
(a) Lactic acid
(b) Carbon dioxide (CO_2)
(c) Oxygen (O_2)
(d) Nitrogen (N_2)

11. During inhalation, what happens to the diaphragm?

(a) It relaxes
(b) It contracts and moves downward
(c) It contracts and moves upward
(d) It remains stationary

12. Which gas is primarily responsible for the feeling of breathlessness at high altitudes?
    (a) Helium
    (b) Oxygen
    (c) Carbon dioxide
    (d) Nitrogen

MULTIPLE CHOICE QUESTIONS (MCQ)-2:

1. Find the incorrect statement from the following:
    (a) Friction on the lung surface is reduced by pleural fluid.
    (b) Complete cartilaginous rings are present in bronchi and initial bronchioles.
    (c) Change in the volume of the thoracic cavity is directly proportional to the volume of lung (pulmonary) cavity. This arrangement is essential for breathing.
    (d) Thin elastic cartilaginous flap (epiglottis) covers the glottis region and prevents the entry of food into the larynx during swallowing.
2. During inspiration
    (a) External intercostals muscles (EICM) and diaphragm become relax.
    (b) Internal intercostals muscles (IICM) and diaphragm become relax.
    (c) External intercostals muscles (EICM) and diaphragm become contract.
    (d) Internal intercostals muscles (IICM) and diaphragm become contract.
3. The volume of air expelled out from the lungs forcefully after a maximum inspiratory effort is called ___.
    (a) Residual volume
    (b) Tidal volume
    (c) Vital capacity
    (d) Total lung volume
4. FRC (Functional residual capacity) can be represented as

(a) TV + IRV+ERV
(b) TV + ERV
(c) RV+ERV
(d) IRV+RV

5. The total thickness of respiratory diffusion membrane is about
   (a) Less than 1 cm
   (b) Less than 1 mm
   (c) Less than 1 nm
   (d) more than 1 mm
6. Which of the following factor causes increase in dissociation of oxyhaemoglobin?
   (a) Free fatty acid concentration in blood falls
   (b) pH of blood falls
   (c) pH of blood rises
   (d) CO_2 concentration in blood falls
7. CO_2 transportation in blood is dependent upon
   (a) Solubility of CO_2 gas in blood.
   (b) Carbonic anhydrase of RBCs.
   (c) Binding of haemoglobin with CO_2.
   (d) Blood proteins.
8. Find the correct statements.
   (a) Negative pressure in lungs causes expiration.
   (b) Tracheal rings are made of hyaline cartilage.
   (c) Sternum is present at the dorsal side of thoracic chamber.
   (d) All the above
9. Which enzyme is responsible for the transportation of CO_2 as bicarbonate in blood?
   (a) Carbonic anhydrase
   (b) Succinic dehydrogenase
   (c) Carboxypeptidase
   (d) Thrombokinase
   (e) Lactase
10. Find the correct statements:
    (a) RBCs help in transportation of oxygen only.
    (b) Both ribs and sternum become lift up due to contraction of internal intercostals muscles (IICM).
    (c) Around 500ml volume of air taken into the lungs during normal inspiration per one heart beat.
    (d) During expiration the interpleural pressure is slightly below the surrounding atmospheric pressure.

ASSERTION AND REASON QUESTIONS:

Read the **assertion** *and* **reason** *carefully to mark the correct option out of the options given below:*

(a) If both the assertion and the reason are true and the reason is a correct explanation of the assertion.
(b) If both the assertion and reason are true but the reason is not a correct explanation of the assertion.
(c) If the assertion is true but the reason is false.
(d) If both the assertion and reason are false.

1. **Assertion:** Closed type of circulatory system is present in mollusca,
   Reason: Haemoglobin is present in mollusca.
2. **Assertion:** Diffusion of CO_2 through the diffusion membrane per unit is much higher than that of O_2.
   Reason: CO_2 has 20 to 25 times more solubility than that of O_2.
3. **Assertion:** Non-collapsible region in respiratory tract of our system are trachea, primary, secondary and tertiary bronchi and terminal bronchioles.
   Reason: These structures are supported by incomplete cartilaginous ring
4. **Assertion:** Breathing pressure in human is negative.
   Reason: In inspiration, air drawn in lungs due to negative pressure in lungs.
5. **Assertion:** The respiratory region of respiratory tract is consisting of alveoli and their duct form.
   Reason: In that region, exchange of O_2 and CO_2 between blood and atmospheric air.
6. **Assertion:** The region in between external nostril and terminal bronchioles is called as both conducting and respiratory zone of respiratory tract.
   Reason: Here atmospheric air enters alveoli of lungs followed by diffusion of gases (O_2 & CO_2) in between blood and atmospheric air.
7. **Assertion:** In inspiration process, alveolar air is released out from lungs.
   Reason: In expiration process, atmospheric air is drawn into the lungs.
8. **Assertion:** The respiratory rate of our body can be altered by pneumotaxic centre can alter.

Reason: Inspiration rate of or body can be reduced due to the neural signal from pneumotaxic centre.

9. **Assertion:** In normal condition, 100 ml of oxygenated blood deliver 5 ml of O_2 to the body tissues.
   Reason: 4ml of CO_2 per 100 ml of deoxygenated blood is delivered into the alveoli.
10. **Assertion:** In humans, Oxygen (O_2) is transported in the form of oxyhaemoglobin.
    Reason: In humans, CO_2 is only transported in the form of carbamino - haemoglobin.

***

Chapter-4: Body fluid and circulation

- **Introduction**
- **Blood**
- **Blood groups**
- **Lymph**
- **Circulatory system**
- **Heart**
- **Cardiac cycle and cardiac output**
- **ECG**
- **Disorders**
- **Golden box**
- **Knowledge points**
- **Multiple choice questions (MCQs)**
- **Assertion & Reason questions**

INTRODUCTION:

Essential substances i.e. Nutrients, O_2 are required in all living cells; while harmful substances are removed from body. In different animal groups, the methods of transport are also different.

Organisms like sponges and coelenterates use water for essential substances and removal of waste substances; while special fluids like blood are used in more complex organisms including human for the same purposes. Lymph is another body fluid which helps in transport of specific substances.

BLOOD (special connective tissue):

Blood= Fluid matrix + Plasma+ formed elements

Plasma:

1) It is 55% of blood, viscous fluid and straw coloured.
2) 90-92% H_2O + 6-8% proteins + small amount minerals (Na^+, Ca^{++}, Mg^{++}, HCO_3^-, Cl^-, etc.)+ Other substances (Glucose, amino acids, lipids, clotting factors etc.).
3) The major proteins are albumins (helps in osmotic balance), globulins (involved in defense mechanisms) and fibrinogen (helps in coagulation of blood).
4) Clotting factors are in inactive form within plasma.
5) Plasma – Clotting factors= Serum

Formed elements (constitute 45%of blood):

RBCs (Erythrocytes)+WBCs (Leucocytes) + Thrombocytes (Blood platelets).

RBCs

a) RBCs are produced from red bone marrow. Its number is about ***5 to 5.5 millions /mm³*** in adult healthy human blood.
b) In most mammals, nucleus is absent and cells are biconcave.
c) ***Haemoglobin*** (so blood become red in colour) is present in RBCs and takes an important role in transportation of respiratory gases. Around ***12 to 16 gram*** of haemoglobin present in 100ml of healthy adult human blood.
d) The life span of RBCs is about 120 days. ***Spleen*** is also known as *graveyard of RBCs*.

WBCs:

a) WBCs are colourless, short life span and its number is about 6000 to 8000/mm^3.
b) Granulocytes and agranulocytes are two types of WBCs. Granulocytes are neutrophils, eosinophils and basophils; while agranulocytes are lymphocytes and monocytes.

c) Neutrophils constitute 60-65 % of the total WBCs and phagocytic in nature.
d) Basophils are about 0.5-1% of total WBCs. These cells produce histamine, serotonin, heparin, etc; which are involved in inflammation.
e) Eosinophils constitute about 2-3% of total WBCs. These cells resist infections and involved in allergic reactions.
f) Lymphocytes constitute 20-25% of total WBCs. Two types of types of lymphocytes i.e. B and 'T lymphocytes and involved in body immune responses.
g) Monocytes constitute about 6-8% of total WBCs and phagocytic in nature.

Thrombocytes

These cells are produced from megakaryocytes (present in bone marrow) and about 1.5 to 3.5 lakhs/mm^3 of adult human blood. These cells produce substances; which are involved in blood clotting (blood coagulation).

GOLDEN BOX- 1:

Write the components and functions of the formed elements in the blood.

The components of formed elements are RBCs, WBCs and Platelets. Haemoglobin present in RBCs, which helps in transportation of oxygen gases. WBCs help in defense mechanism of our body and platelets help in blood clotting mechanism.

Explain about importance of plasma proteins?

Albumins, globulins, fibrinogen, prothrombins are the plasma protein. Among them albumins are the most abundant plasma proteins. This albumin proteins helps in maintenance of fluid in between blood vessels and tissue i.e. maintenance of blood colloidal osmotic pressure. Immunoglobulins help in immune response. Fibrinogen and other clotting factors are involved in clotting mechanism. Plasma proteins bind and transport various substances like hormone, drugs, fatty acids etc. Again, the pH of blood is maintained by plasma proteins. Again plasma proteins provide viscosity to the blood.

Explain blood as a connective tissue?

Blood is mesoderm in origin and consisting of cells (formed elements) and matrix (plasma). Again fibrin appears during blood clotting. So blood is considered as connective tissue.

BLOOD GROUPS:

ABO- Blood Grouping *(figure-1)*:

A-antigens and B-antigens are present on the surface of RBCs. Antigens are the chemicals which induce immune responses and the proteins produced within plasma due to immune response are the antibodies. A, B, AB and O are four types of blood groups (based on the distribution of these antigens and antibodies).

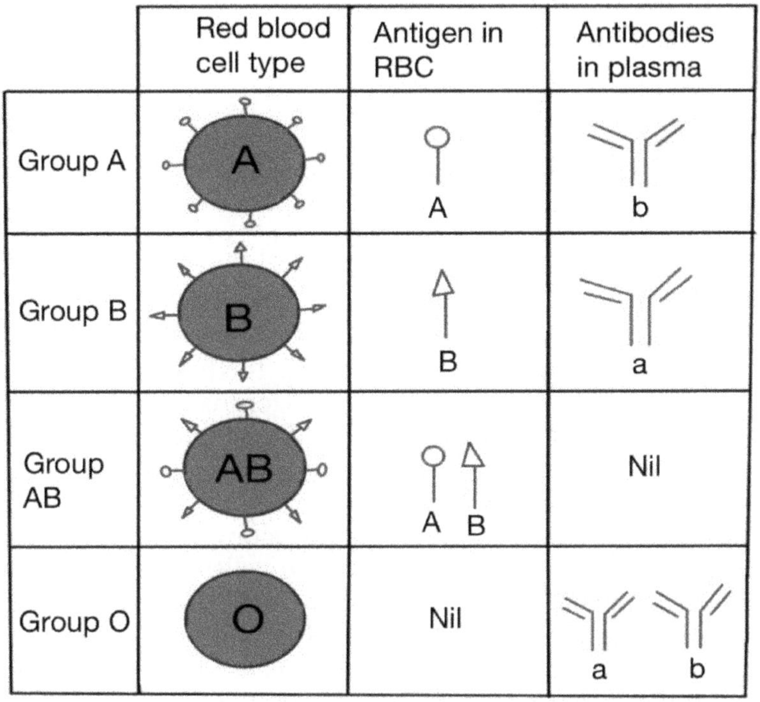

Figure-1: ABO blood group

The blood of both donor and recipient should be matched before blood transfusion, otherwise that may leads to clumping (destruction of RBCs). "O" blood group (can donate blood to any other blood groups) is also called as universal donors. "AB" blood group (can receive blood from any other blood groups) is also called as universal recipients.

Rh blood group

There are two types of Rh-blood groups, on the basis of presence or absence of Rh-antigen on the surface of RBCs i.e. Rh-positive (Rh +ve) and Rh- negative (Rh –ve). Approx. 80% humans have Rh +ve group. Rh

–ve person develop antibodies when exposed to Rh +ve blood and causing clumping due to this mismatching (Rh incompatibility).

When mother is Rh negative and foetus is Rh positive, then Rh antigen is not exposed to Rh antibody during 1st pregnancy and first child is excaped. During parturition, small amount of foetus blood expose to maternal circulation and Rh antibodies developed in mother circulation. That can cause destruction of foetal RBCs in subsequent pregnancy and may fatal to foetus due to severe anaemia and jaundice and called as ***erythroblastosis foetalis***. This condition can be avoided by using anti Rh antibodies.

Blood coagulation (Blood clotting)

This mechanism prevents more loss of blood from body. ***Coagulum*** (clot) is the network of thread (fibrin) develops at the site of injury. It is dark reddish brown colour.

Platelets release certain factors in response to injury or trauma. Tissue injury also causes release of certain factors. These factors activate blood coagulation mechanism. That leads to activation of enzyme complex ***thrombokinase***. This complex helps in conversion of inactive plasma protein prothrombin into active thrombin. In the presence of thrombin enzyme, inactive plasma protein fibrinogen is converted into active fibrins. Fibrins are the network of threads, which helps in coagulation. Calcium ions are the important factors for blood coagulation.

Lymph (Tissue fluid)

In blood capillaries, some amount of water along with small water soluble substances leak into the spaces in between cells of tissues. This released fluid is called as tissue fluid or interstitial fluid. The minerals distribution of this fluid is equivalent to plasma of blood and helps in exchange of nutrients, gases etc. in between blood and cells. This tissue fluid (lymph) is collected by Lymphatic system and drain into major veins.

Lymph is colourless, contains specialized lymphocytes and carrier of nutrients, hormones etc. Lymphocytes help in immunity. Lymph helps in absorption of fats in lacteals.

CIRCULATORY SYSYTEM:

- **Open type:** In this type, heart pumps blood into sinuses (body cavities or open spaces) through large vessels (examples: arthropods, molluscs).
- **Closed type:** In this type, heart pump blood into closed network of blood vessels (Annelids, Chordates)

Heart is muscular in all vertebrates. It is 2 chambered in fishes, 3 chambered in amphibians and reptiles (except crocodiles) and 4 chambered (two atria and two ventricles) in crocodiles, birds and mammals.

In fishes, deoxygenated blood passed through heart (single circulation) and become oxygenated in gills. In amphibians and reptilians, oxygenated blood enter left auricle and deoxygenated blood enter into right auricle of heart. Both the blood become mixed in single ventricle and pumped out from heart (incomplete double circulation). In birds and mammals, there is no mixing of blood (complete double circulation).

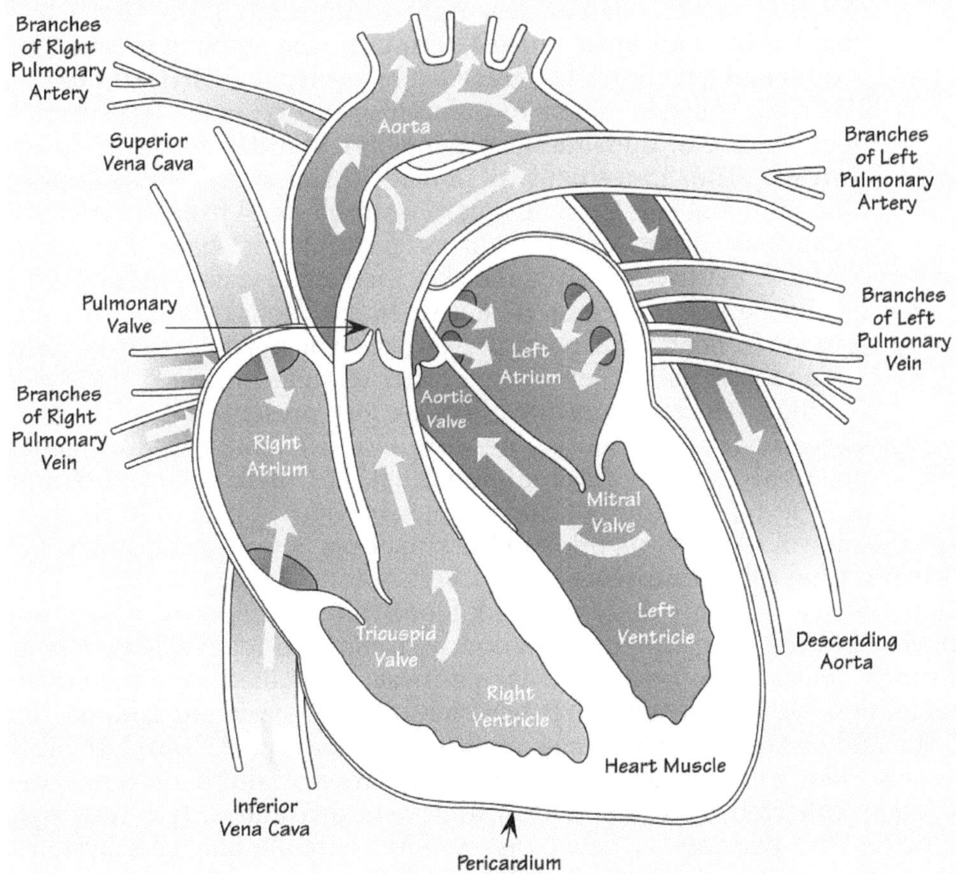

Figure-2: Structure of human heart

HEART *(figure-2)*:

a) Heart is mesodermal in origin, which is present in mediastinum region in between two lungs of thoracic cavity.

b) It is tilted towards left and clenched fist size. Double walled membranous bag protects the heart called as pericardium; which contains pericardial fluid within it.
c) Two small chambers are the atria and two large chambers are the ventricles.
d) Inter atrial septum (thin & muscular wall) separates right and left atria. Inter ventricular septum (thick walled) separate left and right ventricles.
e) Opening present in between right atrium and right ventricle is guarded by ***tricuspid valves***. Similarly, the opening between left atrium and left ventricle is guarded by bicuspid or ***mitral valve***.
f) The right ventricle opens to pulmonary artery; while left ventricle opens to aorta. Both these openings are guarded by ***semi lunar valves***. The movement of blood through valves is always unidirectional (i.e. from atrium to ventricles and from ventricles to pulmonary artery/aorta). Valves prevent the back movement of blood. Ventricular wall is thicker than atrial wall.
g) Cardiac muscle present in entire heart. Nodal tissues are also present in heart. SA node present at right upper corner of right. AV node present at left lower corner of right atrium. Beside this, Bundle of His and Purkinje fibres are also present.
h) These nodal muscular tissues are auto-excitable (produce action potentials without external stimulus) and their action potentials are varying in different nodal system i.e. 70-75 min–1 In SAN; 40 min^{-1} in AVN; 18-25 min^{-1} in Purkinje fires.

Double type of circulation

Right ventricle pump deoxygenated blood into pulmonary artery and moves towards lungs for oxygenation and come to left auricle of heart through pulmonary veins. This pathway is called as pulmonary circulation. Simultaneously, left ventricle pumps oxygenated blood into aorta and move towards tissue of different body parts through blood vessels (like arteries, arterioles and capillaries); where deoxygenated blood is collected by venules, vein and venacava and enters into right auricle. This pathway is called as systemic circulation. This systemic circulation provides nutrients, O2 and other essential substances to tissue. Both pulmonary and systemic circulation is called double type of circulation.

Hepatic portal system: Vascular connection between digestive tract and liver and connection is called as Hepatic portal vein. Then hepatic vein opens to systemic circulation.

GOLDEN BOX- 2:

What is significance of double circulation?

When the circulation of blood takes place in two separate loops is called as double circulation. It is consisting of pulmonary circulation (in between heart and lungs) and systemic circulation (in between heart and remaining body parts). The significances of double type of circulation are

- Heart pump with high pressure at its left side (i.e. high pressure in systemic circulation), so that it can efficiently delivery or transfer of oxygen and nutrients to the tissue.
- Heart pump with low pressure at its right side (i.e. low pressure in pulmonary circulation), so that it prevent the damage in delicate lungs tissue

Explain about the heart of vertebrates on the basis of evolutionary change.

Two chambered heart present in fish (carry deoxygenated blood), three chambered heart present in amphibians and reptiles (except crocodile) and give mixed blood to body parts. But in aves and mammals, four chambered heart is present where no formation of mixed blood. Again single type of circulation is present in fish and incomplete double type of circulation is present in both amphibians and reptiles. Complete double type of circulation is found in aves and mammals. In this way, the complexity of heart increase from fishes to mammals. This represents the evolution of vertebrate's heart.

What is myogenic heart?

When rhythmic impulses are generated within the heart itself and cause contraction. Then, this type of heart is called myogenic heart.

CARDIAC CYCLE & CARDIAC OUTPUT:

Cardiac cycle

Blood flow from pulmonary veins and vena cava to left and right ventricle through left and right atrium. During that period, semi-lunar valve becomes closed. Atrial systole occurs due to the action potential generated from SA node. This atrial systole increases flow of blood up to 30%. During ventricular systole, closing of biscuspid and tricuspid valves takes place along with opening of semi-lunar valves. That leads to flow of blood from ventricles to pulmonary artery and aorta. In ventricular diastole, semi-lunar valves become closed along with opening of bicuspid and tricuspid valves. Again blood flow freely into ventricles. Joint diastole is the state at which both atrium and ventricles are in relaxed state. This events takes place repeatedly in a cyclic manner called as cardiac cycle. In one minute, many cardiac cycles takes place (one cardiac cycle require approximately 0.8 second).

Stroke volume: It is the amount of blood pump out from each ventricle. It is about 70ml.

Cardiac output:

I. Stroke volume (70ml) × Heart beat (72times/minute) = 5040ml/minute = 5 litre/minute (in healthy person).

II. Cariac output can be altered (As both stroke volume and heart beat of body altered). The cardiac output of athlete is much higher than normal person.

During cardiac cycle, 1st heart sound (lub) is generated due to the closing of both bicuspid and tricuspid valves and 2nd heart sound (dub) is generated due to closing of tricuspid valves. Both 1st and 2nd heart sounds have clinical significance.

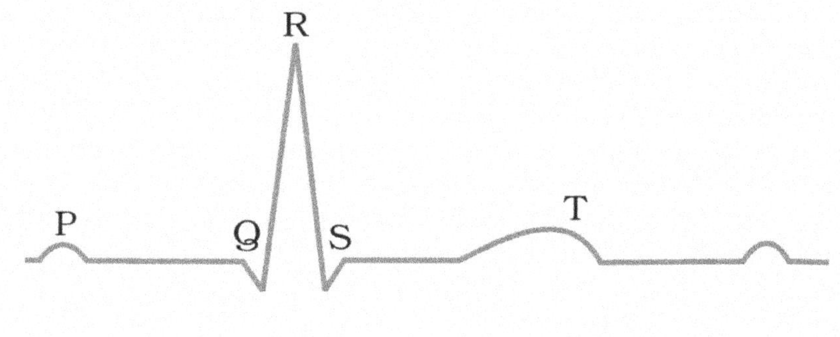

Figure-3: ECG

ECG (Electrocardiogram) *(figure-3)*:

It is the graphical presentation of heart electrical activity during cardiac cycle and the machine is called electrocardiograph. For this, three numbers of electrodes are connected to patient (one on each wrist and one at ankle). There are three peaks in ECG i.e. P wave, QRS complex and T wave. P wave determines atrial depolarization (electrical excitation) i.e. contraction of both atrium. QRS complex determines ventricular depolarization i.e. contraction of both ventricles. T wave determines ventricular repolarisation and marks the end of ventricular systole. Slight deviations from ECG may causes diseases and have great clinical significance.

GOLDEN BOX-3: **Why SA node is called pacemaker in our heart?**

SA node generates electrical impulses and causing heart beat. So it is called as pacemaker.

Explain the significance of AV (atrio-ventricular node) and atrio-ventricular bundle during functioning of heart?

AV node is present left lower part of right atrium. It delays 0.1 seconds, which is essential for the contraction of atria. AV bundles (Bundle of His) arises from AV node and passes through inter-ventricular septum and spread impulses to the ventricles through Purkinje fibres. Both AV node and AV bundles are essential for the coordination of heartbeat. Dysfunction of these structure lead to heart block.

Define a cardiac cycle and the cardiac output.

Cardiac cycle is the sequence of events in heart from beginning of heart beat to another. Each cardiac cycle last for 0.83 seconds (approx. 0.8 second) with heart rate of 72 times/minutes. Cardiac output is the volume of blood removed out from each ventricle per minutes. It is the multiplication of heart beat (72 times/minutes) and stroke volume (70 ml). Its value is about 5 litre/minute

What is heart sounds?

The sound generated in heart during beating is called heart sound. The first heart sound (LuBB).is low pitch and created due to closing of cuspid valves. The second heart sound (Dup) is high pitch and formed due to closing of semi lunar valves.

Explain the different segments of standard ECG?

P wave represents atrial depolarization. QRS represent ventricular depolarization, T wave represent ventricular repolarisation. ST segment represent the time gap between ventricular depolarization and repolarisation.

DISORDERS:

a) **Hypertension (high blood pressure)**
Normal blood pressure is 120/80 mmHg. Here 120 mm Hg is the systolic pressure; while 80mm Hg is the diastolic pressure. If blood pressure of a person is 140/90 or more, then it is considered as hypertension. That causes heart diseases and can affect important organs like kidney, brain.

b) **Coronary artery disease (CAD)**
It is referred as Atherosclerosis. Here Fat, calcium, cholesterol and fibrous tissue become deposited in the lumen of blood vessels (arteries) and make it narrow. In this way supply of blood to heart muscle will be affected.

c) **Angina pectoris** (Acute chest pain)

In this type, not enough oxygen is reaching to heart muscle. This effect is more common in middle aged and elders.

d) Heart failure

Here heart is not pumping blood effectively. It is also called as congestive heart failure. It is different from cardiac arrest (when heart stops beating) or heart attack (damage of heart muscle due to due to inadequate blood supply.

DIFFERENCE BETWEEN:

Blood	Lymph
1. Formed elements (RBCs, WBCs & Platelets) + plasma 2. High plasma proteins 3. Its movement takes place due to pumping of heart. 4. Colour red 5. Transport gases 6. It helps in transportation of oxygen, nutrients and hormones. Again it causes removal of CO2 and waste materials.	1. WBCs (mostly lymphocytes)+ lymph plasma 2. Low plasma proteins 3. Its movement takes place due to contraction of body muscle and valves. 4. Colour clear or slight yellowish 5. No such events 6. It drains interstitial fluid and helps in absorption of fats from intestine.
Open Circulatory System	**Closed Circulatory System**
1. Slow rate of circulation 2. Blood pressure is low 3. Blood is confined to vessels and sinuses 4. Less efficient 5. Insecta, mollusc	1. Fast rate of circulation 2. Blood pressure is high 3. Blood is confined to only vessels 4. More efficient 5. Vertebrates
Systole	**Diastole**
1. Contraction of heart 2. Higher blood pressur 3. Shorter duration 4. Blood pump out	1. Relaxation of heart 2. Lower blood pressure. 3. Longer duration 4. Here blood filled up in heart.
P-wave	**T-wave**

1. Atrial depolarization 2. Access atrial function 3. Before QRS complex	1. Ventricular depolarization 2. Ventricular recovery 3. After QRS complex

KNOWLEDGE POINTS:

- Normal heart beat and rate of breathing can be established by ***CPR*** (Cardiopulmonary resuscitation) procedure. Standard CPR is the combination of cardiac compression and artificial ventilation. But hand only CPR is the preferred method.
- ***Pericarditis*** is the inflammation of pericardium. Acute pericarditis is most common type and can persist about 1 week. Drug like aspirin can reduce this inflammation.
- ***Myocarditis*** is the inflammation of myocardium and symptomless. This occurs due to viral infection, rheumatic fever, exposure to medicine etc. In severe case condition, it can cause cardiac failure.
- ***Endocarditis*** is the inflammation of endocardium by bacteria and involves heart valves. Fever, fatigue, loss of appetite, night sweats, heart murmur etc. are the symptoms. Intravenous antibiotics are the treatment
- ***Ductus arteriosus*** is a temporary blood vessel connects pulmonary trunk and systemic aorta in foetal stage. After parturition, this blood vessel becomes close and leaving a remnant part known as ***ligamentum arteriosum***.
- When the opening of heart valves become narrow and blood flow become restricted, then it is called ***stenosis***.
- In ***Myocardial ischemia***, blood flow to the coronary artery is partially obstructed.
- The volume of blood ejected from left ventricle into systemic aorta in one minute is called as Cardiac output (CO) i.e. about 5 liters/minute in adult. It is the multiplication of stroke volume and heart rate. The volume of blood ejected out from each ventricle per one heart beat is called stroke volume (SV), which is about 70ml. In mild exercise, the cardiac output can increase to 10 liters/minute. In excessive exercise, the cardiac output can increase near to 20 liters/minute, which is four times larger than in its normal case.

- ***Arrhythmia*** (dysrhythmia) is the abnormal rhythm of heart beat due to defect in its conducting system. Factors like stress, caffeine etc. is responsible for arrhythmia. Dizziness, shortness of breath, chest pain etc. are the symptoms.
- ***Bradycardia*** is the slow heart rate i.e. less than 50 beats per minute. Tachycardia is rapid heart rate i.e. more than 100 beats per minute. Fibrillation is the uncoordinated and rapid heartbeat.
- When AV (atrioventricular) node is block due to rapid regular atrial contractions (240-360 beats/min) is called as atrial flutter.
- In older adults, atrial pumping may ceases due to asynchronous contraction of atria fibres. This type of arrhythmia is called as ***atria fibrillation***. ***Ventricular fibrillation*** is most deadly type of arrhythmia where ventricular fibres are completely asynchronous. Coronary artery diseases are responsible for ventricular fibrillation. This is due to inadequate blood flow to the heart. Here P wave, QRS complexes or T wave are not clearly defined in ECG.
- When structure or function of ventricle is impaired, that can leads to a progressive disorder called as ***Cardiomyopathy***.

MULTIPLE CHOICE QUESTIONS (MCQ-1)

1. Adult human RBCs are enucleated. Which of the following statement(s) is/are most appropriate explanation for this feature?
   I. They are somatic cell
   II. They do not need to reproduce
   III. All their internal space is available to transport oxygen
   IV. They do not metabolize
   (a) I, II, and IV
   (b) III and IV
   (c) Only III
   (d) Only I
2. Blood pressure in the pulmonary artery is
   (a) More than that in the carotid
   (b) Same as that in the aorta
   (c) Less than that in the venae cavae
   (d) More than that in the pulmonary vein

3. This blood vessel in mammals would typically carry the largest amount of urea
   (a) Dorsal aorta
   (b) Renal vein
   (c) Hepatic portal vein
   (d) Hepatic vein
4. How do parasympathetic neural signals affect the working of the heart?
   (a) Both heart rate and cardiac output increase
   (b) Reduce both heart rate and cardiac output
   (c) Heart rate is increased without affecting the cardiac output
   (d) Heart rate decreases but cardiac output increases
5. Which of the following is not a component of the cardiovascular system?
   (a) Heart
   (b) Blood vessels
   (c) Lungs
   (d) Blood
6. Which of the following is the correct sequence of events during the cardiac cycle?
   (a) Atrial systole, ventricular systole, isovolumetric relaxation, ventricular diastole
   (b) Ventricular diastole, atrial systole, ventricular systole, isovolumetric relaxation
   (c) Isovolumetric relaxation, atrial systole, ventricular diastole, ventricular systole
   (d) Ventricular systole, atrial systole, isovolumetric relaxation, ventricular diastole
7. Which of the following is the hormone responsible for regulating blood pressure and volume?
   (a) Aldosterone
   (b) Antidiuretic hormone
   (c) Angiotensin II
   (d) Atrial natriuretic peptide
8. Which of the following is the term used to describe the force exerted by blood against the walls of blood vessels?
   (a) Blood pressure
   (b) Heart rate
   (c) Stroke volume

(d) Cardiac output

9. Which of the following components is responsible for the clotting of blood?
   (a) Platelets
   (b) Red blood cells
   (c) White blood cells
   (d) Plasma
10. In which blood vessel does the exchange of gases occur in the circulatory system?
   (a) Veins
   (b) Arteries
   (c) Capillaries
   (d) Aorta
11. Which of the following hormones is responsible for regulating blood glucose levels?
   (a) Insulin
   (b) Thyroxine
   (c) Estrogen
   (d) Testosterone

MULTIPLE CHOICE QUESTIONS (MCQ-2):

1. Given below are four statements (1 to 4) regarding human blood circulatory system.
   (A) Arteries are thick walled and have narrow lumen as compared to veins.
   (B) Angina is acute chest pain when the blood circulation to the brain is reduced.
   (C) Persons with blood group AB can donate blood to any person with any blood group ABO system.
   (D) Calcium ions play a very important role in blood clotting.

   Which of the above two statements are correct?
   (a) A & D
   (b) A & B
   (c) B & C
   (d) C & D
2. The haemoglobin content per 100 ml of blood of a normal healthy human adult is
   (a) 5 – 11 mg
   (b) 25 – 30 mg

(c) 17 – 20 mg
(d) 12 – 16 mg

3. If due to some injury the chordae tendineae of the tricuspid valve of the human heart is partially non-functional, what will be the immediate effect?
    (a) The flow of blood into the aorta will be slowed down.
    (b) The 'pacemaker' will stop working.
    (c) The blood will tend to flow back into the left atrium.
    (d) The flow of blood into the pulmonary artery will be reduced.
4. Person with blood group AB is considered as universal recipient because he has
    (a) Both A and B antigens on RBC but no antibodies in the plasma.
    (b) Both A and B antibodies are in the plasma.
    (c) No antigen on RBC and no antibody in the plasma.
    (d) Both A and B antigens in the plasma but no antibodies.
5. How do parasympathetic neural signals affect the working of the heart?
    (a) Reduce both heart rate and cardiac output.
    (b) Heart rate is increased without affecting the cardiac output.
    (c) Both heart rate and cardiac output increases.
    (d) Heart rate decreases but cardiac output increases.
6. Erythropoiesis starts in
    (a) Kidney
    (b) Liver
    (c) Spleen
    (d) Red bone marrow
7. Which one of the following is correct?
    (a) Plasma = Blood – Lymphocytes
    (b) Serum = Blood + Fibrinogen
    (c) Lymph = Plasma + RBC + WBC
    (d) Blood = Plasma + RBC + WBC + Platelets
8. Doctors use stethoscope to hear the sounds produced during each cardiac cycle. The second sound is heard when:
    (a) Ventricular walls vibrate due to gushing in of blood from atria
    (b) Semilunar valves close down after the blood flows into vessels from ventricles

(c) AV node receives signal from SA node
(d) AV valves open up

9. Which of the following correctly explains a phase/event in cardiac cycle in a standard electrocardiogram?
   (a) The QRS complex indicates atrial contraction.
   (b) The QRS complex indicates ventricular contraction.
   (c) The time between S and T represents atrial systole
   (d) The P–wave indicates the beginning of ventricular contraction.
10. The cardiac impulse is initiated and conducted further up to ventricle. The correct sequence of conduction of impulse is
   (a) SA Node → AV Node → Purkinje fibres → AV Bundle
   (b) SA Node → Purkinje fibres → AV Node → AV Bundle
   (c) SA Node → AV Node → AV Bundle → Purkinje fibres
   (d) SA Node → Purkinje fibres → AV Bundle → AV Node

ASSERTION AND REASON QUESTIONS:

Read the **assertion** *and* **reason** *carefully to mark the correct option out of the options given below:*

(a) If both the assertion and the reason are true and the reason is a correct explanation of the assertion.
(b) If both the assertion and reason are true but the reason is not a correct explanation of the assertion.
(c) If the assertion is true but the reason is false.
(d) If both the assertion and reason are false.

1. **Assertion:** The more effective circulatory system is closed type.
   Reason: Speed and efficiency of circulation is considerably enhanced in closed type circulatory system.
2. **Assertion:** During exercise, cardiac output increases.
   Reason: Oxygen consumption is less during cardiac output.
3. **Assertion:** The openings of both pulmonary artery and systemic aorta are guarded by valves.
   Reason: The backward flow of blood in ventricles is prevented by these valves.
4. **Assertion:** Sinu Auricular node is also called as pacemaker of heart.
   Reason: This node causes both initiation and maintenance of heart rhythm.
5. **Assertion:** Out of four chambers of human heart, the wall of left ventricle is thicker one.

Reason: The pumping of blood takes place throughout our body from left ventricle.

6. **Assertion:** Universal donors are the 'O' blood group individuals.
   Reason: Antigens are absent on the surface of RBCs in 'O' blood group individuals.
7. **Assertion:** In first pregnancy, Erythroblastosis foetalis cannot observe (foetus is Rh positive and mother is Rh negative).
   Reason: In first pregnancy, Rh antigens of foetus do not get exposed to Rh negative blood of mother.
8. **Assertion:** Contraction of both atria and ventricle do not occur simultaneously.
   Reason: This is due to AV nodal delay.
9. **Assertion:** Semi lunar valves become closed during starting of ventricular diastole.
   Reason: Ventricular pressure becomes decrease during ventricular diastole.
10. **Assertion:** If nerve supply to human heart becomes cut off, then there are no changes in heart beat.
    Reason: The heart of human is myogenic.

***

Chapter-5: Excretory Products and its Elimination

- **Introduction**
- **Human excretory system**
- **Physiology of excretion**
- **Regulation**
- **Micturition**
- **Role of other organs in excretion**
- **Disorders**
- **Golden box**
- **Knowledge points**
- **Multiple choice questions (MCQs)**
- **Assertion & Reason questions**

INTRODUCTION:

The nitrogenous waste products (Ammonia, Urea, Uric acid), CO_2, water, ions like (Na^+, K^+, Cl^-, phosphate, sulphate, etc.) are produced due to metabolic activities or excess intake. These substances should be removed from our body either totally or partially.

a) Ammonotelism:
It is the process in which removal of ammonia takes place from our body. Ammonia is readily soluble, more toxic and its removal required with maximum loss of water (Many bony fishes, aquatic amphibians and aquatic insects).

b) Ureotelism: Urea is produced from ammonia within liver of mammals, many terrestrial amphibians and marine fishes. Urea is removed from our body with moderate loss of water.

c) Uricotelism: Uric acid excretes in the form of pellet or paste from reptiles, birds, land snail and insects. Uric acid is less toxic and removed with very less amount water loss.

Protonephridia or flame cells: This excretory structure is present in platyhelminthes (planaria), rotifers, some annelids and cephalochordates (Amphioxus). Protonephridia helps in osmoregulation.

Nephridia: It is tubular structure and maintains a fluid and ionic balance (e.g. Earthworm and other annelids).

Malpighian tubules:
This structure helps in osmoregulation and removal of nitrogenous waste products (Insects).

Antennal glands (green lands): This excretory structure are present in crustaceans (like prawns).

GOLDEN BOX-1:

What is osmoregulation?
The process in which living organisms maintain water and solutes balance in our body is called as osmoregulation. This process is essential to our body because too much water and salts or too little water and salts can cause shrink or burst of cells. In this way, cell function becomes disrupted (e.g. kidney of human).

Why the excretory substances in terrestrial animals are generally either urea or uric acid, but not ammonia?
Ammonia is highly toxic and highly reactive than urea and uric acid. So its removal need large amount of water. Urea is less toxic and its removal required moderate amount of water. Uric acid is least toxic and it is removed in the form of paste or solid. So many aquatic animals are ammonotelic types. Again terrestrial animals are either

ureotelic or uricotelic types.

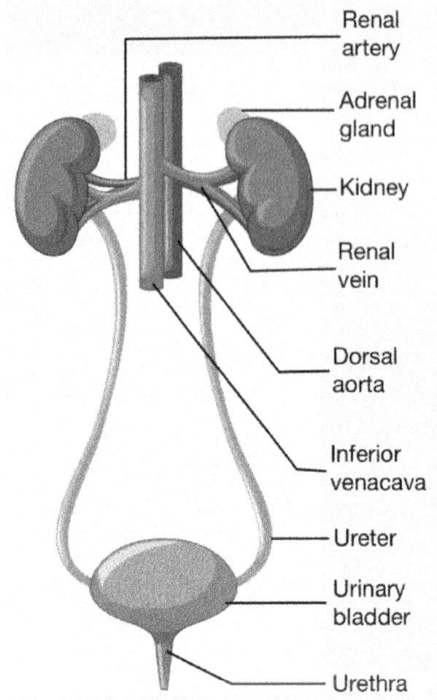

Figure-1: Human excretory system

HUMAN EXCRETORY SYSTEM *(Figure-1)*:

Human excretory system is consisting of kidney (1 pairs), ureter (1 pairs), urinary bladder and urethra.

Kidney *(Figure-2)*:

Kidney is Bean shaped, reddish brown colour and present in between last thoracic and 3rd lumbar vertebrae. Length, width and thickness of each adult kidney are about 10-12 cm, 5-7 cm and 2-3 cm respectively. Its concave surface has a structure called as hilum. Ureter, blood vessels and nerve centre enter into kidney through hilum.

Nephrons are the functional unit of Kidney. Around 10 lakhs numbers of nephrons are present in each kidney. Glomerulus and renal tubule are the two components of each nephron.

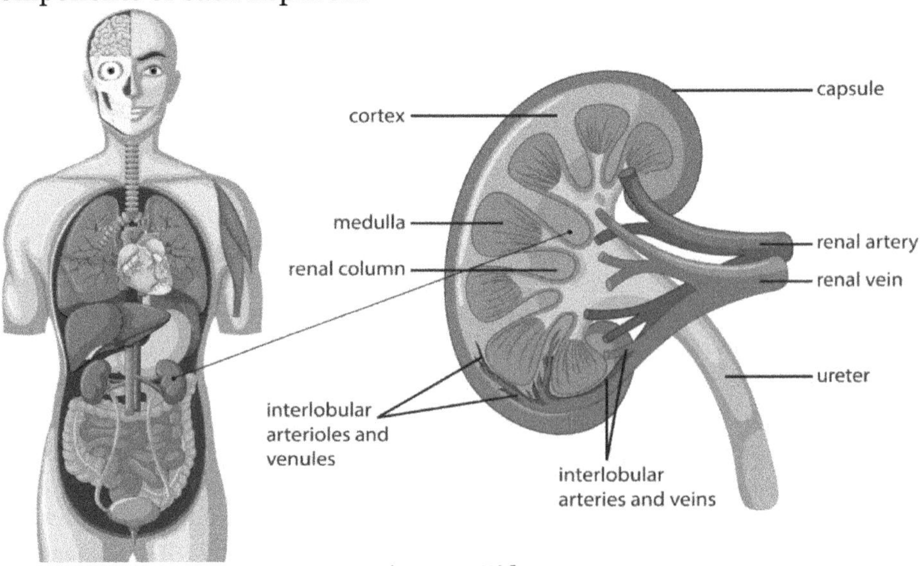

Figure-2: Kidney

Glomerulus is a network of capillaries formed by afferent arterioles and opens to efferent arterioles. Renal tubule begins with Bowman's capsule (which enclose glomerulus) and continue with PCT (proximal convoluted tubule), Loop of Henle and DCT (Distal convoluted tubule). Malpighian body is the combination of Glomerulus and Bowman's capsule.

DCT of many nephrons opens to collecting duct. Collecting ducts open to medullary pyramids followed by calyces and renal pelvis. In the cortical region, malpighian corpusceles, PCT and DCT of nephrons are present; while in medulla region, loop of Henle is present. Loop of Henle is short in cortical nephrons and very long in juxta medullary nephrons. Peritubular capillaries (produced from efferent arterioles) are the fine network of capillary and present around renal tubules. Vasa recta is network like structure and its minute vessel becomes U shaped and parallel to loop of Henle. This network structure is highly reduced or absent in cortical nephrons.

PHYSIOLOGY OF EXCRETION:

Urine formation:

Ultra filtration/Glomerular filtration, Selective reabsorption and tubular secretion are the processes of urine formation.

Ultra filtration:

Filtration takes place through glomerular capillaries. These capillaries have 3 layers i.e. endothelium of glomerular blood vessels (inner), basement membrane (middle) and epithelium of Bowman's capsule (outer). Glomerular capillary blood pressure causes ultra filtration. Around 1100-1200 ml of blood ($1/5^{th}$ of stroke volume) per minute undergoes filtration.

GFR (glomerular filtrate rate) is the filtrate produced from kidneys per minute. It is about 125ml/minute (or 180 liter/day) in healthy individual. JGA (Justa glomerular apparatus) carried out the mechanism which helps in regulation of GFR. JGA is formed by cellular modification of DCT (macula densa) and afferent arterioles (JG cells) at the point of their contact. When GFR decreases, JG cells become activate and release renin. Renin brings GFR back to normal by stimulating glomerular blood flow.

Selective reabsorption:

It is estimated that nearly 99% of glomerular filtrate become reabsorbed by renal tubules and the process is called as selective reabsorption. The remaining percentage is removed from body in the form of urine (1.5 litres). Either active (glucose, amino acids, Na+ etc.) or passive (nitrogenous waste, water) transport mechanism takes place during reabsorption process.

Tubular Secretion:
Substances like H+, K+ and ammonia are secreted from tubular cells and helps in urine formation. In this way, ionic and acid base balance of body fluid is maintained.

GOLDEN BOX-2:

What is Glomerular Filtration Rate (GFR) and explain its autoregulatory mechanism?

The amount of filtrate formed in our kidney per unit time after ultrafiltration is called glomerular filtrate rate (GFR).In normal case, its value is about 125ml/minutes (180 litres/day). Through GFR, we can diagnose the stages of chronic kidney diseases and monitor the kidney functions.

The ***autoregulatory mechanism of GFR*** includes myogenic mechanism and JGA. In myogenic mechanism, the smooth muscles of afferent arterioles become contract during increase in blood pressure. That prevents sudden rise in GFR. Again afferent arterioles become relax during decrease in blood pressure. This allows more blood into the glomerulus and maintains GFR. On the basis of JGA, Increase in GFR causes vasoconstriction at afferent arteriole. In this way, GFR reduce back to normal. Decrease in GFR causes vasodilation at afferent arterioles and stimulate the release of renin. In this way, GFR increased into normal level.

What is significance of JGA (juxta glomerular apparatus) in kidney?

JGA is consisting of JG cells, macula densa and mesanglial cells. This apparatus is regulating blood pressure through RAAS mechanism, homeostasis of sodium and fluid balance.

Functions of the Tubules:

PCT :

Almost all nutrients are absorbed in PCT (due to increase in surface area as it is lined with simple cuboidal brush border epithelium)

a) Around 70-80% of electrolytes and water are reabsorbed in PCT
b) Both pH and ionic balance of body fluid is maintained by secretion of hydrogen ions, ammonia and potassium ions from PCT.

Loop of Henle

The descending part of loop of Henle is permeable to water, but almost impermeable to electrolytes. The filtrate becomes concentrated in downward direction.

The ascending part of loop of Henle (minimum reabsorption) is permeable to Na^+(actively) and Cl^- (passively), but impermeable to water.

Filtrate becomes diluted in upward direction. Ascending limb helps in maintenance of high osmolarity at medullary interstitial fluid.

DCT

Selective Reabsorption of Na+ takes place conditionally (by active transport mechanism) with the influence of aldosterone hormone. Similarly, reabsorption of water takes place conditionally (by passive mechanism) with the influence of ADH hormone. Again, HCO_3^- also reabsorbed in DCT region.

Na-K and pH of the blood become maintained due to secretion of H^+, K^+ and NH_3.

Collecting duct

Inside kidney, this duct extends from cortex to inner part of medulla and responsible for reabsorption of large amount of water. In this way, this duct helps in the formation of concentrated urine.

a) Small amount of urea released from this duct (at inner medullary region) and keep the osmolarity at medullary interstitial region.
b) Again, tubular secretion of hydrogen and potassium ions take place at collecting duct region and helps in maintenance of pH and ionic balance inside blood.

REGULATION:

Both hypothalamus and JGA are directly involved in the regulation of kidney functioning along with heart (up to some extent).

(I)Hypothalamus: Activated osmoreceptors (due to loss of body fluid) stimulate hypothalamus to release ADH/vasopressin from neurohypophysis and responsible for water reabsorption in later part of tubules. In this way, diuresis is prevented.

a) Changes in blood volume, body fluid volume and ionic concentration cause activation of osmoreceptors.
b) ADH is also responsible for constrictor effects on blood vessels followed by increase in blood pressure, increase in glomerular blood flow and increase in GFR.

(II)JGA (Responsible for Renin-Angiotensin mechanism):

If GFR/ glomerular blood pressure/ glomerular blood flow decreases, then JG cells become activated and causes the release of renin hormone.

a) ***Renin*** is responsible for conversion of angiotensinogen to angiotensin-I followed by angiotensin-II. This ***angiotensin-II*** causes release of aldosterone from adrenal cortex.
b) Aldosterone is responsible for reabsorption of Na+ and water from distal part of tubules and causes increase in blood pressure followed by GFR.

(III)Heart: When blood flow increases to the atria of heart, then ***Atrial natriuretic factor*** (ANF) released from heart. This factor causes vasodilation followed by decrease in blood pressure. This mechanism checks renin-angiotensin mechanism.

MICTURITION:

Urinary bladder is in stretching condition due to filling of urine. Stretch receptors present in the wall of urinary bladder and send signal to the CNS followed by release of voluntary signal (passes through motor nerve cells) from CNS. This voluntary signal is responsible for simultaneous events i.e.

a) Contraction of smooth muscle present in urinary bladder.
b) Relaxation of urethral sphincter

Both events are responsible for release of urine called as micturition. And the reflex is called as micturition reflex.

Urine of human is light yellow in colour, slightly acidic (pH-6) and has odour. In humans, around 1 to 1.5 litres urine (containing 25 to 30 gram of urea) is produce per day. Many disorders (like glycosuria, ketonuria) and malfunctioning of kidney can be clinically diagnosed through analysis of urine.

GOLDEN BOX-3:

What is counter current mechanism?

Counter current mechanism helps in concentration of urine and conservation of water. This mechanism occurs in loop of Henle and vasa recta of juxtamedulary nephrons. In loop of Henle, descending limb is permeable to water but not salts, while ascending limb is permeable to salts but not water. Vasa recta act as counter current exchanger and maintain concentration gradient. This mechanism creates and maintains hyperosmolarity at medulla region of kidney. This medullary gradient allows water reabsorption in collecting duct with the influence of ADH and this leads to concentration of urine.

What is the role of liver, lungs and skin in excretion?

Liver, lungs, skin are the other excretory organs. In liver, different functions takes place i.e. deamination of amino acids, urea synthesis, detoxification of harmful substances (drugs, alcohol) and bile production (Bilirubin is waste products). Through lungs, CO_2 gas (200ml/minute) and water vapour (400ml/day). Skin contains both sweat glands and sebaceous glands. Both sweat and sebum are removed from our body

What is Micturition?

The physiological process of urination is called micturition. When urinary ladder is filled with urine (around 300 to 400ml), stretch receptors of urinary bladder become activated and send signal to CNS. Then micturition reflex become activated. In this way, smooth muscle of urinary bladder become contract and internal sphincter (involuntary) become relax. But we can hold the urine by controlling external sphincter. When both the sphincters are relaxed, then urination takes place.

ROLE OF OTHER ORGANS IN EXCRETION:

Skin, lungs and liver are the other organs which are also responsible for the elimination of excretory waste products.

a) Skin contains both sweat glands (produce sweat) and sebaceous glands (produce sebum). *Sweat* is responsible for cooling effect and helps in removal of some of its components. NaCl, urea (small amount), lactic acids etc. are the components of sweat. *Sebum* provides protective oil covering to ***skin*** and consisting of sterols, hydrocarbons and waxes.
b) CO_2 (200ml/minute approx.) is removed from our ***lungs*** along with significant amount of water.
c) Bilirubin, biliverdin, cholesterol, vitamins, drugs and degraded part of steroid hormones are the components of *bile* (produced from largest gland of our body i.e. ***Liver***) and eliminated from our body along with digestive waste.

DISORDERS:

Uremia: This condition developed due to accumulation of urea in blood (malfunctioning of kidney) and causes kidney failure. The solution is hemodialysis and kidney transplantation.

a) In ***hemodialysis***, blood is allowed to enter into the cellophane tube (coiled and having pores) with the addition of heparin and this tube is surrounded by dialyzing fluid. This fluid has same composition with that of plasma but do not have nitrogenous waste products. This tube helps in passage molecules based on concentration gradient. This clear blood pumped backed into vein after addition of antiheparin.
b) In ***kidney transplantation***, donor functional kidney of close relatives is used to prevent rejection by host immune system. Now a days, this transplantation success rate is increased due to modern clinical procedure.

Renal calculi: Crystal salts like oxalate in the form of stone or insoluble mass are formed within the kidney.

Glomerulonephritis: Glomerular Inflammation within kidney.

DIFFERENCE BETWEEN:

Cortical Nephron	Juxta-medullary Nephron
1. This type of nephrons constitutes 85% of total nephrons.	1. This type of nephrons constitutes 15% of total nephrons.
2. Here Loop of Henle is short.	2. Here Loop of Henle is long.
3. Here Peritubular capillaries are present.	3. Here Vasarecta is present.
4. It is present mostly in cortex region of kidney.	4. It is present at cortico-medullary junction region of kidney.
5. Here glomerulus is smaller.	5. Here glomerulus is larger.

KNOWLEDGE POINTS:

- Kidneys are ***retroperitoneal*** because its position is posterior to the peritoneum of abdominal cavity. Both 11th and 12th ribs protect kidneys partially. If there is fracture in lower ribs, that can leads to puncture in kidney followed by life threatening damage. Due to presence of liver, right kidney is slightly lower than left kidney.
- If adipose capsule (renal fascia) becomes deficient, Kidneys become slip out from its normal position. This kind of defect is called ***Nephroptosis***. Here urine flow can be blocked and even pain arises due to twisting of ureter. It is more common in female than male.
- If glomerular capillaries become damaged, plasma proteins can lose through urine and causes edema (abnormal high volume interstitial fluid).
- ***Glucosuria*** is the condition in which some glucose remain in urine because absorption of glucose cannot be takes place properly due to increase in glucose level more than 200 mg/ml in blood. It can causes polyuria, decreased blood volume, dehydration.

MULTIPLE CHOICE QUESTIONS (MCQs)-1:

1. A decrease in blood pressure/volume will not cause the release of
   (a) ADH
   (b) Renin
   (c) Atrial natriuretic factor
   (d) Aldosterone
2. Pick the correct statement
   (a) Ascending limb of loop of Henle is impermeable to water
   (b) Descending limb of loop of Henle is impermeable to water
   (c) Ascending limb of loop of Henle is permeable to water
   (d) Descending limb of loop of Henle is permeable to electrolytes
3. Typically, human urine is acidic as
   (a) Hydrogen ions are actively secreted into the filtrate
   (b) Sodium transporter exchanges one hydrogen ion for each sodium ion, in peritubular capillaries
   (c) Excreted plasma proteins are acidic
   (d) Potassium and sodium exchange generates acidity
4. Maximum amount of electrolytes and water, about 70-80%, from the glomerular filtrate is reabsorbed in which part of the nephron?
   (a) Proximal convoluted tubule
   (b) Ascending limb of loop of Henle
   (c) Descending limb of loop of Henle
   (d) Distal convoluted tubule
5. A fall in glomerular filtration rate (GFR) activates.
   (a) Posterior pituitary to release vasopressin
   (b) Adrenal medulla to release adrenaline
   (c) Juxtaglomerular cells to release renin
   (d) Adrenal cortex to release aldosterone
6. This is a common characteristic observed in both human beings and adult frog
   (a) Ureotelic mode of excretion
   (b) Internal fertilization
   (c) Nucleated RBCs
   (d) Four-chambered heart
7. This amongst the following correctly explains the function of a specific part of the human nephrons
   (a) Afferent arteriole – carries blood away from glomerulus towards the renal vein

(b) Distal convoluted tubule – reabsorption of K^+ ions into the surrounding blood capillaries
(c) Henle's loop – most reabsorption of the major substances from the glomerular filtrate
(d) Podocytes – create minute spaces for filtration of blood into the Bowman's capsule

8. The region at which both nerves and blood vessels enter the kidneys is called ____.
   (a) Hilum
   (b) Tubules
   (c) Pelvis
   (d) Medulla
9. Which of the following is responsible for the formation of Columns of Bertini?
   (a) Medulla
   (b) Renalpelvis
   (c) Calyces
   (d) Cortex

MULTIPLE CHOICE QUESTIONS (MCQs)-2:

1. Why human urine is usually acidic?
   (a) Excreted plasma proteins are acidic
   (b) Potassium and sodium exchange generates acidity
   (c) Hydrogen ions are actively secreted into the filtrate
   (d) The sodium transporter exchanges one hydrogen ion for each sodium ion, in peritubular capillaries.
2. In mammals, which blood vessel would normally carry largest amount of urea?
   (a) Renal Vein
   (b) Dorsal Aorta
   (c) Hepatic Vein
   (d) Hepatic Portal Vein
3. The part of nephron involved in active reabsorption of sodium is
   (a) Proximal convoluted tubule
   (b) Bowman's capsule
   (c) Descending limb of Henle's loop
   (d) Distal convoluted tubule
4. Find the correct statements related to kidney function regulation.
   (a) Exposure to cold temperature stimulates ADH release.

(b) An increase in glomerular blood flow stimulates the formation of angiotensin II.
(c) During summer when the body loses lot of water by evaporation, the release of ADH is suppressed.
(d) When someone drinks lot of water the ADH release is suppressed.

5. If glomerular filtration rate (GFR) decrease, then it activates _____.
(a) Adrenal cortex to release aldosterone
(b) Adrenal medulla to release adrenaline
(c) Posterior pituitary to release vasopressin
(d) Juxtaglomerular cells to release rennin

6. Find the correct categorization of given animals according to the type of nitrogenous wastes {A (Ammonotelic), B (Ureotelic), C (Uricotelic)} they give out?
(a) A: Frog, Lizards, B: Aquatic Amphibia, Humans, C: Cockroach, Pigeon
(b) A: Aquatic Amphibia, B: Frog, Humans, C: Pigeon, Lizards, Cockroack
(c) A: Aquatic Amphibia, B: Cockroach, Humans, C: Frog, Pigeon, Lizards
(d) A: Pigeon, Humans, B: Aquatic Amphibia, Lizards, C: Cockroach, Frog

7. Find the correct statement related to excretion in human kidneys.
(a) Descending limb of Loop of Henle is impermeable to water.
(b) Distal convoluted tubule is incapable of reabsorbing HCO_3^-.
(c) Nearly 99 per cent of the glomerular filtrate is reabsorbed by the renal tubules.
(d) Ascending limb of loop of Henle is impermeable to electrolytes.

8. The principal nitrogenous excretory compound in humans is synthesized
(a) In kidneys but eliminated mostly through liver.
(b) In kidneys as well as eliminated by kidneys.
(c) In liver and also eliminated by the same through bile.
(d) In the liver, but eliminated mostly through kidneys.

9. Find out the incorrect statements.
(a) Birds and land snails are uricotelic animals.

(b) Mammals and frogs are ureotelic animals.
(c) Aquatic amphibians and aquatic insects are ammonotelic animals.
(d) Birds and reptiles are ureotelic.

10. Find out the incorrect statements.
    (a) The medullary zone of kidney is divided into a few conical masses called medullary pyramids projecting into the calyces.
    (b) Inside the kidney the cortical region extends in between the medullary pyramids as renal pelvis.
    (c) Glomerulus along with Bowman's capsule is called the renal corpuscle.
    (d) Renal corpuscle, Proximal Convoluted Tubule (PCT) and Distal Convoluted Tubule (DCT) of the nephron are situated in the cortical region of kidney.

ASSERTION AND REASON QUESTIONS:

Read the **assertion** *and* **reason** *carefully to mark the correct option out of the options given below:*

(a) If both the assertion and the reason are true and the reason is a correct explanation of the assertion.
(b) If both the assertion and reason are true but the reason is not a correct explanation of the assertion.
(c) If the assertion is true but the reason is false.
(d) If both the assertion and reason are false.

1. **Assertion:** Nephridia are the excretory organ in earthworm, which helps in osmoregulation.
   Reason: This excretory structure maintains both fluid and ionic balance in earthworm.
2. **Assertion:** In prawn, antennal glands are the excretory structure.
   Reason: In crustacean, malpighian tubules help in osmoregulation.
3. **Assertion:** Ultrafiltration is the Glomerular filtration.
   Reason: All constituents of blood plasma are filtered finely into lumen of Bowman's capsule except proteins.
4. **Assertion:** In PCT, nitrogenous wastes are absorbed passively.
   Reason: Here absorption is taking place through diffusion process against concentration gradient.
5. **Assertion:** Uricotelic organisms are terrestrial in adaptation.

Reason: These organisms are least toxic and require minimum water for its excretion.

6. **Assertion:** In humans, micturition process is not an endocrine mechanism.
   Reason: Micturition is the process in which urination takes place.
7. **Assertion:** All nutrients along with 70 to 80% of water and electrolytes from glomerular filtrate are reabsorbed in PCT.
   Reason: Brush border epithelium is present in PCT.
8. **Assertion:** Concentration of urine takes place due to counter-current mechanism.
   Reason: The concentration gradient in medullary region of human kidney is maintained by counter-current mechanism.
9. **Assertion:** Human blood pressure can be increased due to aldosterone hormone.
   Reason: Absorption of sodium ion and water takes place in distal part of tubules due to influence of aldosterone hormone.
10. **Assertion:** Both osmotic pressure and composition of glomerular filtrate are equivalent to protein free plasma.
    Reason: This is due to impermeable nature of glomerular capillary wall and inner membrane of Bowman's capsule against large molecules like proteins.

***

Chapter-6: Locomotion and Movement

- **Introduction**
- **Muscle**
- **Mechanism of muscle contraction**
- **Skeletal system**
- **Disorders**
- **Golden box**
- **Knowledge points**
- **Multiple choice questions (MCQs)**
- **Assertion & Reason questions**

INTRODUCTION:

Both animals and plants show movement. Movement in the form of streaming also takes place inside protoplasm of amoeba (unicellular organism). In many organisms, cilia, flagella and tentacles help in movements. Change in place or location can also causes movements. Locomotion is the voluntary movements. Forms of locomotory movements are walking, flying, running, climbing etc.

a. Cilia (Paramoecium) help in both locomotion and movement of food through cytopharynx.
b. Tentacles (Hydra) are also help in both locomotion and capturing prey.
c. Limbs (human being) are also used for both locomotion and change in body posture.

All locomotions are movements but not vice-versa. On the basis of habitats and demand of situation, animals show different mode of locomotion. Locomotion is generally used for shelter, mate, search for food, escape from enemy etc.

Types of movements

Muscular, ciliary and amoeboid movements are present in human body.

a) Macrophage, leucocytes and microfilaments are involved in amoeboid movements.
b) Most of the internal tubular organs of human being are lined with ciliated epithelium like ciliary movements in trachea (help in removal of dust particles) and fallopian tube of female reproductive tract (help in passage of ova).
c) Limbs, jaws, tongue etc. of our body need muscular movements. Movements in human being including locomotion require effective use of muscles.

Coordination activity of muscular, skeletal and neural system leads to locomotion.

MUSCLE:

Swimming of spermatozoa, canal system of sponges (maintain water current) and locomotion of protozoans (like Euglena) show flagellar movements. Muscles constitute 40 to 50% of total human body weight. Excitability, extensibility, elasticity and contractility are the properties of muscles.

On the basis of location, muscles are categorized into three type i.e.

a) ***Skeletal muscle:*** This muscle is closely associated with skeleton of body, voluntary and primarily involved in body posture changes.

b) ***Visceral muscle:*** nonstriated; involuntary; helps in transportation of food and gametes through digestive tract and genital tract respectively)

c) ***Cardiac muscle:*** This muscle present in heart. Its muscle cells are in branching pattern and involuntary in function).

On the basis of appearance, it is generally categorized into two types i.e.

I. ***Striated muscle:*** It is also called as stripped and includes both skeletal muscle and cardiac muscle.

II. ***Non striated muscle*** *(smooth like appearance)****:*** This muscle also called as unstripped muscle and includes visceral muscle.

GOLDEN BOX-1:
What are the different types of movements exhibited by the cells of human body?
Three main types of movements take place in human body i.e. amoeboid, ciliary and muscular movements. Leukocytes and macrophage show amoeboid movement. These are the immune cells, which migrates towards the injury or infection sites. Trachea and fallopian tube show ciliary movements. In trachea, cilia remove the dust particles; while in fallopian tube, cilia helps in movement of ovum within it. Majority of our body movements are the muscular movements.

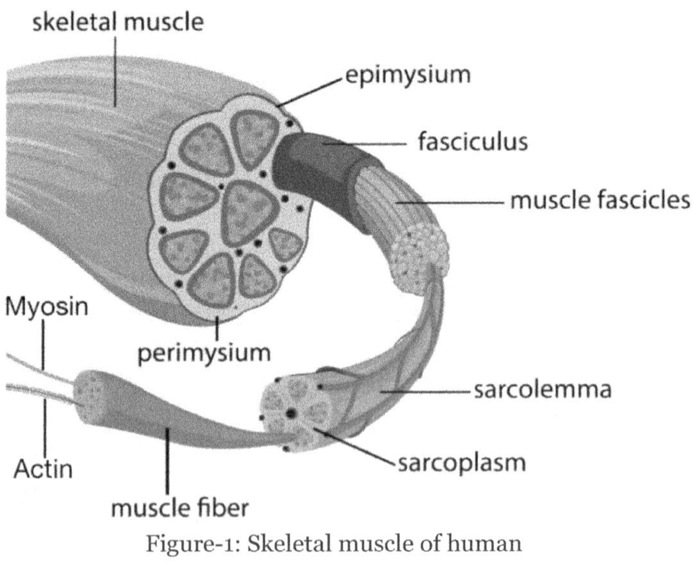

Figure-1: Skeletal muscle of human

Skeletal muscle *(figure-1)*:
Skeletal muscle of human body is consisting of fascicles (number of muscle bundles). These fascicles are bind together by collagenous connective tissue called as fascia. Each muscle bundle is consisting of number of ***muscle fibres***. The membrane, cytoplasm and endoplasmic reticulum of each muscle fibre (syncitium) called as sarcolemma, sarcoplasm and sarcoplasmic reticulum respectively.
Myofilaments (also called as ***myofibrils***; large in numbers) are the parallelly arranged filaments found in sarcoplasm of muscle fibre. Alternate dark (contain myosin; Anisotropic/A band) and light bands (contain actin protein; isotropic/I bands) are present in each myofibril. Both Actin and Myosin are proteins and responsible for striated appearance.
These proteins are rod like, parallel to themselves and also longitudinal axis of myofibrils. Actin filaments are thin filaments while myosin filaments are thick filaments. Z line present is in I band, while M line is present in the A band. The region in between two Z line is called as sarcomere (functional unit of contraction). Thin filament slightly overlaps with thick filament at resting stage. The part of myosin, which is not overlapped by myosin, is called as H zone.

Structure of Contractile Proteins:

Actin/Thin filament:
This filament is consisting of two numbers of filamentous or F-actins (helically arranged), tropomyosins (two filaments) and troponin.

a) F-actin is consisting of monomeric globular or G actin.
b) Tropomyosins are run close to F-actins.
c) Troponins are present at regular interval on tropomyosin and mask the active binding site or myosin.

Myosin/Thick filament:
Each thick filament (polymerized protein) is consisting of many monomeric protein called as meromyosin.

a) Each meromyosin is consisting of heavy meromyosin i.e. HMM (globular head with short arm) and light meromyosin i.e. LMM (tail).
b) Short arm projected outwards in HMM at regular interval called as cross arm.
c) Both ATP binding site and actin binding sites are present in globular head.

MECHANISM OF MUSCLE CONTRACTION:

Sliding filament theory:

According to this theory, muscle fibre contraction is due to sliding of thin filaments over thick filament. Signal produced from CNS is transported through motor neurons and responsible for muscle contraction. A motor neuron along with muscle fibre is called ***motor unit***. Neuromuscular (***motor end plate***) junction is the junction in between motor neuron and sarcolema of muscle fibre.

- ***Neurotransmitters*** (Acetyl choline) are the chemical, which are released from motor-end plate after induced by neural signal and responsible for the formation of action potential in sarcolemma. This action potential reaches to the sarcoplasmic reticulum after spreading to the muscle fibre and responsible for the opening of voltage gated calcium channel. That causes increase in the level of calcium ions within sarcoplasm.
- ***Calcium ions*** bind with subunit of troponin on actin filaments and responsible for removal of mask site at actin filament for myosin. That causes the binding of head of myosin to the active site on actin myofilament with the utilization of energy (ATP) and form cross bridge.
- This ***cross bridge*** pulls the actin myofilament towards the centre A band. That causes inward pulling of Z line and responsible for shortening or contraction of sarcomere.
- During muscle contraction, I band become reduced while A band remain same in length. Then both ADP and Pi released from myosin during relaxed state. Then cross bridge become broken after the binding of ATP.
- When calcium ions returned back into cisternae part of sarcoplasic reticulum, then muscle contraction become stop followed return back of Z line to its original position and masking of actin filament.

Muscle fatigue: This type of condition developed due to repeated muscle activation followed by accumulation of ***lactic acid***. Lactic acid formed due to anaerobic respiration of glycogen.

Red fibres (Aerobic muscle): This type of muscle is reddish in appearance due to high level of myoglobin protein. Level of mitochondria in this muscle is also high and helps in ATP production.

White fibres (anaerobic muscle): This type of muscle is whitish or pale in colour due to very less amount of myoglobin protein.

Again the level of sarcoplasmic reticulum in this muscle is high.

GOLDEN BOX-2:

What is sliding filament theory?

The sliding filament theory represents muscle contraction and formation of force. This theory explained that how actin myofilament (thin filaments) slides over the myosin myofilament (thick filament) and causes shortening of sarcomere. Nerve impulse is responsible for the release of Ca^{2+} from sarcoplasmic reticulum. When Ca^{2+} attach to troponin, the binding site on actin become exposed. Then the binding of head of myosin takes and form cross-bridges. In this mechanism ATP required. Here, there are no changes in the length of actin and myosin. But Z- line becomes closed, that leads to shortening of muscle fibres.

How muscle contraction takes place?

The important steps for muscle contractions are Action potential. Neuromuscular conduction (Here, Action potential arrive at axon terminal) and followed by release of neurotransmitter. Acetyl choline attach to nicotine receptor of muscle fibre and causing influx of Na^+ ion (depolarisation).

- Action potential is transmitted through sarcolemma followed by release of Ca^{2+} into cytoplasm and binding to troponin C.
- Cross bridge formation in between myosin head and active site of actin. Actin filaments are pulled towards centre.
- Myosin head is detached from actin.
- Relaxation phase.

SKELETAL SYSTEM *(figure-2)*:

Human skeletal system has important role in body movements and is consisting of specialised connective tissue i.e. bone (206 numbers in adult) and few cartilages. Calcium salts present in bone matrix. So bone become very hard and non pliable. Chondroitin salts are present in cartilage matrix and make it slightly pliable.

Divisions of human bones: Bone has two principal divisions i.e. Axial; present at) and Appendicular skeleton (126 bones).

***Axial skeletons (80 bones)*:** This type of skeletons are present at the main axis of body and consisting of skull (22 bones), vertebral column (26 bones), sternum (single bone) and ribs (24 bones).

Both cranial (8 numbers) and facial (14 numbers) bones are the two sets of bones present in skull. Cranial bones form hard covering i.e. cranium of brain. Facial bones are the front part of skull.

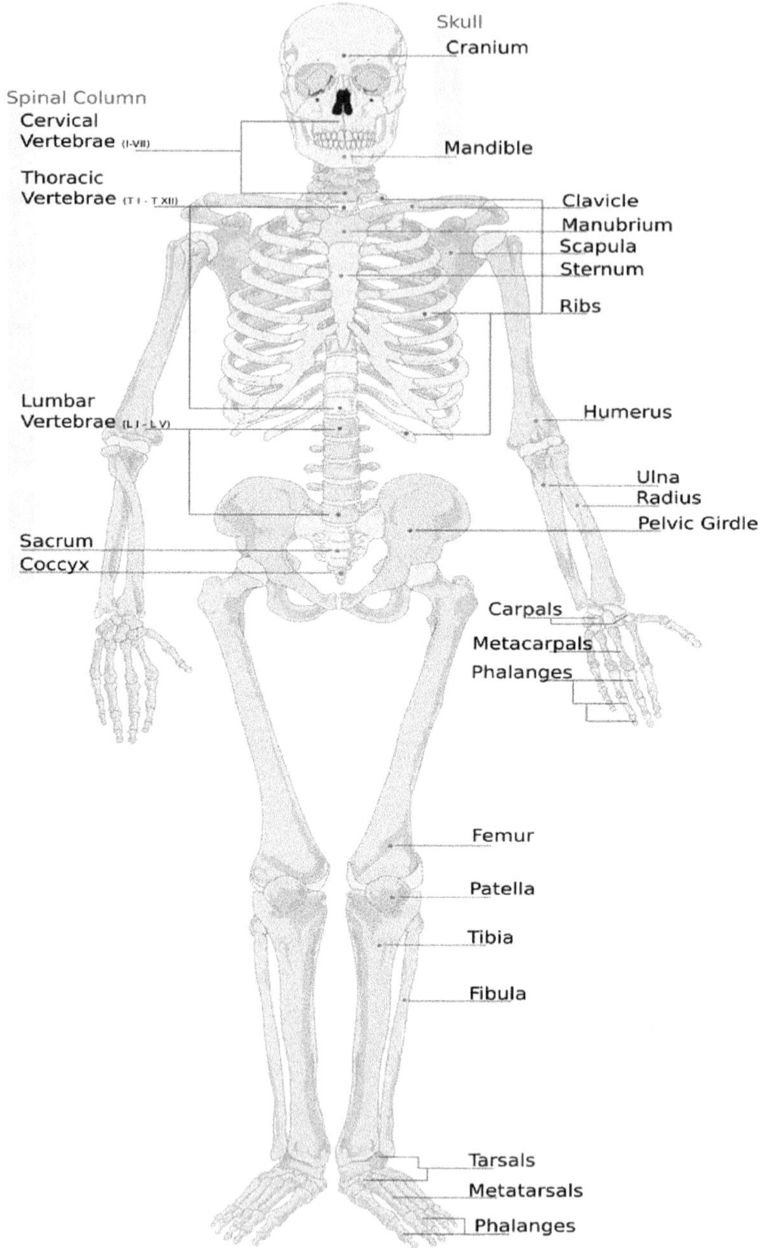

Figure-2: Human skeletal system

Hyoid bone (single and U shaped) is present at the base of buccal cavity and belongs to skull. Malleus, Incus and Stapes (three tiny ear bones/ossicles) are present in each ear.
The articulation in between both skull and vertebral column contains two occipital condyles. So skull in human is ***dicondylic*** type.
Vertebral column is consisting of vertebrae and is the main components of trunk and present dorsally.
Atlas is the first vertebrae and articulate with occipital condyles. Cervical (7 numbers), thoracic (12 numbers), lumber (5 numbers), sacral (1, fused form) and coccygeal (1, fused form) are the different types of vertebrae present in vertebral column.
Almost all mammals including human being have 7 numbers of cervical vertebrae. Vertebral column is the attachment site for both ribs and back musculature. Besides this, vertebral column protects the spinal cord and support head.
Sternum (flat bones) is present at ventral midline thorax. Ribs connect both vertebral column (dorsally) and sternum (ventrally). Each rib is bicephalic (two surface of articulation) on dorsal surface. Three types ribs i.e. true ribs, false ribs and floating ribs.

- True ribs (first 7 pairs) connect both vertebral column and sternum by hyaline cartilage.
- False ribs (8th, 9th and 10th pairs) connect vertebral column at one side and 7th ribs at another side by hyaline cartilage. So this type can also be called as vertebrochondral ribs
- Floating ribs (11th, 12th pairs) become free at ventral side.

Thoracic cage: It is formed by the combination of thoracic vertebrae, ribs and sternum.

Appendicular skeleton

Appendicular skeleton is consisting of limb bones (2 forelimbs and 2 hind limbs; total 120 numbers of bones) and girdles bones (2 pectoral girdles and 2 pelvic girdles; total 6 numbers of bones). Each forelimb is consisting of 30 bones. Similarly, each hindlimb is consisting of 30 bones.
Each ***fore limb*** is consisting of humerus (1), radius (1), ulna (1), carpals (8), metacarpals (5) and phalanges (14). Each ***hind limb*** is consisting of femur (1), tibia (1), fibula (1), patella (cup shaped & cover ventrally, 1), tarsals (7), metatarsals (5) and phalanges (14).
Each ***pectoral girdle*** is consisting of scapula (large, triangular, flat; present at dorsal side; in between 2nd and 7th ribs; 1) and clavicle (long,

slender, with two curvature, also called collar bone; 1). A spine is present in scapula and its expanded process is called acromian (articulate with clavicle). Glenoid cavity is present below acromian and articulate with hea of humerus.

Pelvic girdle is consisting of two coxal bones. Each coxal bone is consisting of ilium, ischium and pubis. Acetabulum (articulate with thigh bone) is the cavity present at the fusion of these bones. Both coxal bones meet ventrally and consisting of white fibrous cartilage i.e. pubic symphysis.

Joints:

The point of contacts between cartilages and bones or between bones is called joints. Joint acts as fulcrum because its movement is carried out by force generated from muscle. Fibrous, cartilaginous and synovial are the three types of joints

a) Fibrous joints (sultures of skull bones) are consisting of dense fibrous connective tissue and do not show any movements.
b) Cartilaginous joints (in between vertebrae of vertebral column) are consisting of cartilage and show limited movements.
c) Synovial joints (between articular surfaces of two bones) have fluid filled synovial cavity and causes considerable movements including locomotion.
    i. *Ball and socket joint:* in between humerus and pectoral girdle, in between femur and pelvic girdle.
    ii. *Hinge joint:* In knee joints, In between phalanges.
    iii. *Pivot joint:* In between atlas and axis
    iv. *Gliding joint:* In between carpals, in between tarshals.
    v. *Saddle joint:* In between carpal an metacarpal of thumb

DISORDERS OF MUSCULAR AND SKELETAL SYSTEM

a) ***Myasthenia gravis*** (auto immune disorder) affect neuromuscular junction and responsible for paralysis, fatigue and weakening of skeletal muscle.
b) ***Muscular dystrophy*** (genetic disorder) is responsible for degeneration of skeletal muscle.
c) ***Tetany*** occurs due to decrease in calcium level in the blood and is responsible for rapid muscular spasm.
d) ***Arthritis*** occurs due to joint inflammation.
e) ***Osteoporosis*** (age related disorder) causes decrease in bone mass and can increase the chances of bone fracture. This defect commonly occurs due to decrease in estrogen level.

f) ***Gout*** is the inflammation of joint. This occurs due to deposition of uric acid in the form of crystals.

DIFFERENCE BETWEEN:

Actin	Myosin
1. Lighter or Isotropic band (I) 2. Slide over myosin and helps in muscle contraction 3. Thin filament 4. It is consisting of globular proteins (i.e. F-actins), tropomyosin and troponins. 5. This myofilament does not show ATPase activity.	1. Darker or Anisotropic band (A) 2. Bind to actin and helps in pulling of actin towards M-line during muscle contraction. 3. Thick filament 4. It is consisting of myosin molecules. Each myosin molecule has a long tail and head regions. 5. This myofilament shows ATPase activity.
Red Muscles	**White Muscles**
1. These muscles are red in colour due to presence of more myoglobin contents. 2. The level of mitochondria is more and can show aerobic respiration. 3. The level of sarcoplasmic reticulum is less. 4. These muscles are resistant to fatigue. 5. The speed of this muscle contraction is slow and can sustain for more time. 6. These muscles help in maintenance of body posture.	1. These muscles are pale yellow in colour due to presence of less myoglobin contents. 2. The level of mitochondria is less and can show anaerobic respiration. 3. The level of sarcoplasmic reticulum is more. 4. These muscles are not resistant to fatigue. 5. The speed of this muscle contraction is fast and short lived. 6. These muscles help in generation of short burst power.
Pectoral Girdle	**Pelvic Girdle**
1. It is consisting of clavicle and scapula	1. It is consisting of Ilium, ischium and pubis.

2. It is present at shoulder region and support forelimbs. 3. Pectoral girdle (scapula) attached to skeleton via muscles; while clavicle connects to the manubrium part of sternum. 4. It helps in arm movements.	2. It is present at hip region and support hindlimbs. 3. Pelvic girdles attached themselves by pubic symphysis and attached to axial skeleton firmly. 4. It is more stable and helps in weight bearing.
Skeletal muscle	**Cardiac muscle**
1. Muscle fibre is Multinucleated 2. Absence of intercalated disc. 3. Muscle fibre is long, cylindrical and unbranched. 4. Fatigue can takes place	1. Muscle fibre is uninucleated 2. Presence of intercalated disc. 3. Muscle fibre is short and branched. 4. No fatigue

KNOWLEDGE POINTS:

- Muscular hypertrophy is the condition in which muscular growth takes place after birth due to enlargement of existing muscle fire. Here the level of mitochondria, sarcoplasmic reticulum, myofibrils etc. becomes increased.
- **Muscular atrophy** is the condition in which the size of muscle fibre becomes decreased. This is due to loss of myofibrils.
- After the death of an individual, ATP synthesis ceases. Again calcium ions leak into sarcoplasm from sarcoplasmic reticulum that leads to binding myosin head to actin. So muscle cannot contract or stretch (rigidity). This condition is called rigor mortis. It starts 3 to 4 hours after death and last for 24 hours. Then cross bridge is digested by proteolytic enzymes of lysosomes.
- The electrical activity of muscles at resting or contracting stages is determined by test called as ***Electropmyography***.

No electrical activity during resting stage.

- ❖ When muscle tone lost or decreased, then it is called hypotonia. Here muscle is in flaccid condition (loose and flattened). When muscle tone increased, then it is called ***hypertonia***
- ❖ Pain associated with muscle is called myalgia. Tumor in muscle tissue is called as ***Myoma***. Inflammation of muscle fibre is called ***Myositis.***
- ❖ Increase in muscular excitability and contractility and relaxation decreased. Then this condition is called as ***Myotonia.***

MULTIPLE CHOICE QUESTIONS (MCQs)-1:

1. The pivot joint between atlas and axis is a type of
   (a) fibrous joint
   (b) synovial joint
   (c) saddle joint
   (d) cartilaginous joint
2. Which ion is responsible for unmasking of active sites for myosin or cross-bridge activity during muscle contraction?
   (a) Potassium
   (b) Magnesium
   (c) Calcium
   (d) Sodium
3. Lack of relaxation between successive stimuli in sustained muscle contraction is known as
   (a) Fatigue
   (b) tonus
   (c) tetanus
   (d) spasm
4. At which region, motor neuron stimulate a muscle fiber?
   (a) The sarcoplasmic reticulum
   (b) The myofibril
   (c) The transverse tubules
   (d) The neuromuscular junction
5. Find the correct statement with regards to locomotion in humans
   (a) Accumulation of uric acid crystals in joints causes their inflammation

(b) A decreased level of progesterone causes osteoporosis in old people
(c) Joint between adjacent vertebrae is a fibrous joint
(d) Vertebral column has 10 thoracic vertebrae

6. In skeletal muscle fibers, H-zone is formed due to
(a) The central gap between myosin filaments in the A-band
(b) Absence of myofibrils in the central portion of A-band
(c) Extension of myosin filaments in the centre portion of the A-band
(d) Central gap between actin filaments extending through myosin filaments in the A-band

7. Muscle contraction in human is due to
(a) Actin filaments shorten.
(b) A, I and H bands shorten.
(c) A band remains the same.
(d) Sarcomere does not shorten

8. Find the correct statement with regards to specific disorder of muscular or skeletal system.
(a) Gout – inflammation of joints due to extra deposition of calcium.
(b) Muscular dystrophy – age-related shortening of muscles.
(c) Osteoporosis – decrease in the bone mass and higher chances of fractures with aging.
(d) Myasthenia gravis – an autoimmune disorder which inhibits sliding of myosin filaments

9. This is the correct description of a certain part of a normal human skeleton.
(a) Glenoid activity is a depression to which the thigh bone articulates.
(b) First vertebra is axis which articulates with the occipital condyles.
(c) The 9th and 10th pairs of ribs are called the floating ribs.
(d) Parietal bone and the temporal bone of the skull are joined by fibrous joint

MULTIPLE CHOICE QUESTIONS (MCQs)-2:

1. The sliding filament theory can be best explained as
(a) When myofilaments slide pass each other actin filaments shorten while myosin filaments do not shorten.

(b) Actin and myosin filaments shorten and slide pass each other.
(c) Actin and myosin filaments do not shorten but rather slide pass each other.
(d) When myofilaments slide pass each other, the myosin filaments shorten while actin filaments do not shorten.

2. Glenoid cavity articulates
(a) Clavicle with acromion
(b) Scapula with acromion
(c) Clavicle with scapula
(d) Humerus with scapula
3. Which of the following joints would hallow no movement?
(a) Cartilaginous joint
(b) Synovial joint
(c) Ball and socket joint
(d) Fibrous joint
4. Coccyx is formed by the fusion of :-
(a) 3 vertebrae
(b) 5 vertebrae
(c) 4 vertebrae
(d) 6 vertebrae
5. Acetabulum is formed by :-
I. ilium
II. ischium
III. pubis
(a) I, II
(b) I, III
(c) I, II, III
(d) II, III
6. Find the correct statement with respect to locomotion in humans.
(a) A decreased level of progesterone causes osteoporosis in old people.
(b) Accumulation of uric acid crystals in joints causes their inflammation.
(c) The vertebral column has 10 thoracic vertebrae.
(d) The joint between adjacent vertebrae is a fibrous joint.
7. Find out incorrect statement.
(a) Heart muscles are striated and involuntary.
(b) The muscles of hands and legs are striated and voluntary.

(c) The muscles located in the inner walls of alimentary canal are striated and involuntary.
(d) Muscles located in the reproductive tracts are unstriated and involuntary.

8. Find out true statement.
   (a) Head of humerus bone articulates with the acetabulum of pectoral girdle.
   (b) Head of humerus bone articulates with the glenoid cavity of pectoral girdle.
   (c) Head of humerus bone articulates with a cavity called acetabulum of pelvic girdle.
   (d) Head of humerus bone articulates with a glenoid cavity of pelvic girdle.
9. Muscles with characteristic striations and involuntary nature are
   (a) Muscles in the wall of alimentary canal.
   (b) Muscles of the heart.
   (c) Muscles assisting locomotion.
   (d) Muscles of the eyelids
10. Find out incorrect options.
    (a) Hinge joint – Present between humerus and pectoral girdle
    (b) Pivot joint – Present between atlas, axis and occipital condyle
    (c) Gliding joint – Present between the carpals
    (d) Saddle joint – Present between carpal and metacarpal of thumb

ASSERTION AND REASON QUESTIONS:

Read the assertion *and* reason *carefully to mark the correct option out of the options given below:*

(a) If both the assertion and the reason are true and the reason is a correct explanation of the assertion
(b) If both the assertion and reason are true but the reason is not a correct explanation of the assertion
(c) If the assertion is true but the reason is false
(d) If both the assertion and reason are false

1. **Assertion**: The example of mobile joints is Ball and socket joints.
   Reason: In synovial cavity, synovial fluid is present which helps in considerable movement.
2. **Assertion**: Our joint becomes painful after inflammation.

Reason: Here inflammation occurs due to deposition of toxic substances.

3. **Assertion**: The changes in our body posture are due to the body parts movement.
   Reason: Body parts movement takes place on the basis of body axis.
4. **Assertion**: Locomotion in unicellular organisms and multicellular animal has similarities.
   Reason: In unicellular animals, ciliary, flagellar and amoeboid movements are found.
5. **Assertion**: Simple type of movement present in amoeba.
   Reason: In amoeba, streaming of protoplasm takes place.
6. **Assertion**: In hydra, tentacles are present and show multiple functions.
   Reason: Tentacles of hydra helps in locomotion and capturing of prey.
7. **Assertion**: Amoeboid movement takes place in macrophages and leucocytes in blood.
   Reason: Here, pseudopodia can form due to streaming of protoplasm
8. **Assertion**: Dust particle and some foreign substances; which are inhaled along with the atmospheric air during inspiration can be removed from trachea
   Reason: Ciliated epithelium is present in trachea.
9. **Assertion**: Muscle contraction occurs due to calcium ions.
   Reason: In actin myofilament, calcium ion binds to the subunit of troponin and responsible for removal of masking at the active sites for myosin
10. **Assertion**: Most of our internal tubular organs are lined with ciliated epithelium and show ciliary movement characteristics.
    Reason: In female reproductive tract, passage secondary oocyte takes place due to ciliary movement.

***

Chapter-7: Neural Control and Coordination

- **Introduction**
- **Human neural system**
- **Nerve conduction**
- **Central neural system**
- **Knowledge points**
- **Golden box**
- **Multiple choice questions (MCQs)**
- **Assertion & Reason questions**

INTRODUCTION:

The process in which organs (two or more) interact and complement functions with each other called as Coordination. During physical exercise, Muscles, lungs, heart, blood vessels, kidney and other organs are coordinated.

a) During physical exercise, muscular activity increases. That causes increase in demand of energy along with the demand of oxygen supply. So increase in oxygen supply needs increase in rate of respiration, heart beat and increase in blood flow.
b) The activities of nerves, lungs, heart and kidney are in normal state at the ending of physical exercise.

Neural system and Endocrine system are coordinated in synchronized fashion in our body.

Neural system of human (organized network connection) is responsible for quick coordination and includes transmission of nerve impulse, impulse across synapsis and reflex action.

Neurons are the specialised cells, which can detect, receive and transmit different stimuli.

(a) In lower invertebrates, this system is very simple (e.g.: Hydra)
(b) In Insects, this system is better organized and contains brain, some ganglia and neural tissue.
(c) In vertebrates, this system is more developed.

HUMAN NEURAL SYSTEM:

Human neural system is consisting of central neural system i.e. CNS (Brain and spinal cord) and peripheral neural system i.e. PNS (somatic neural system i.e. SNS and autonomic neural system i.e. ANS). Sympathetic and parasympathetic neural system are the components of ANS.

(i) CNS is the site of control and information processing.
(ii) Afferent and efferent fibres are the nerve fibres of PNS. Afferent fibres help in passage of nerve impulses from peripheral organs or tissue to CNS; while efferent fibres help in passage of nerve impulses from CNS to peripheral organs or tissue.
(iii) SNS helps in relay of nerve impulses from CNS to skeletal muscle; While ANS helps in passage of nerve impulses from CNS to involuntary organs and smooth muscles.

(iv) Visceral nervous system (part of PNS) includes fibres, ganglia, plexuses and complex nerves. This nervous system helps in passage of nerve impulses from CNS to viscera and vice versa.

Neuron *(figure-1)*

Cell body, dendrites (short fibres) and axon (long fibre) are the three components of neuron.

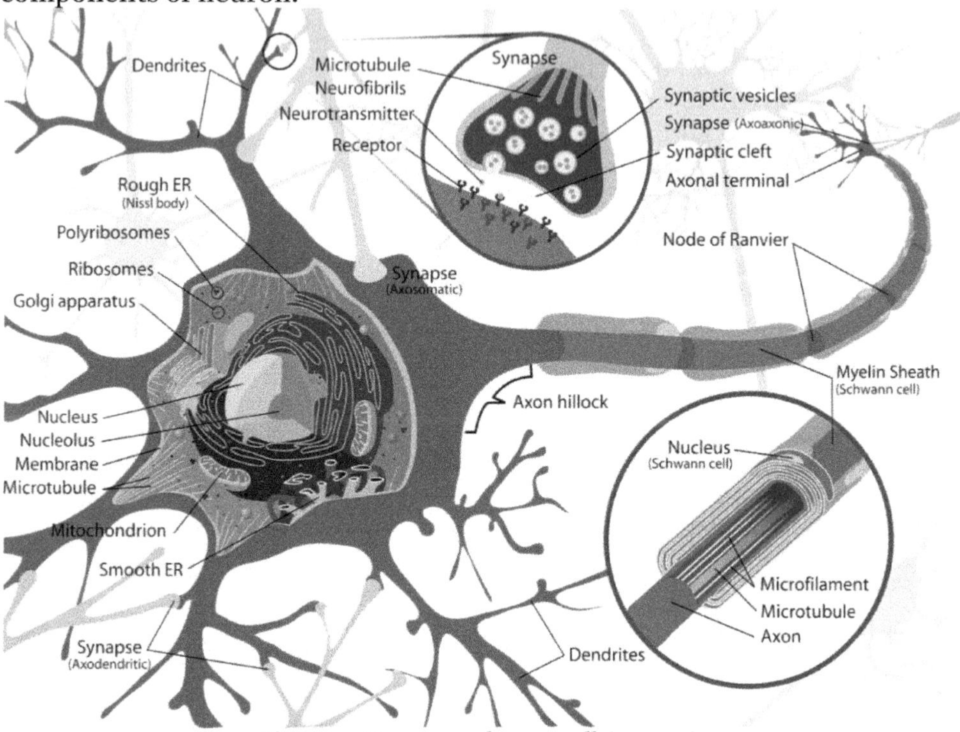

Figure-1: Structure of nerve cell (neuron)

- Cell organelles and Nissle's granules (granular bodies) are present in cytoplasm of cell body. Nissle's granules are also present in dendrites. Dendrites help in passage of nerve impulses towards cell body.
- Axon is branched at its distal end and each branch terminates as synaptic knob (bulb like structure). Synaptic vesicles (containing neurotransmitters) are present in synaptic knob. Nerve impulses transmitted by axons towards synapse or neuromuscular junction.

- Myelinated and nonmyelinated are two types of axons. Schwann cells produce myelin sheath around axon of myelinated nerve fibre (having nodes of Ranvier and present in both cranial and spinal nerves. In nonmyelinated nerve fibre (present in autonomous and somatic neural system), Schwann cells present, but donot produce myelin sheath

On the basis of numbers of dendrites and axon, neurons are three types i.e.

a) ***Multipolar neurons:*** This type neuron contains one axon and two or more dendrites along with cell body. e.g. present in cerebral cortex.
b) ***Bipolar neurons:*** This type of neuron contains one axon and one dendrite along with cell body. E.g. present in retina of eye.
c) ***Unipolar neurons:*** This type neuron contains only one axon along with cell body. e.g. present at embryonic stage.

NERVE CONDUCTION:

Generation and Conduction of Nerve Impulse: The membrane of neuron contains different ion channels, which are selectively permeable to different ions.

a) Axoplasm contains more concentration of K+ ions and negatively charged proteins, while ECF (extra cellular fluid i.e. outside the axon), contains more concentrations of Na+ ions and less concentration of K+ ions.
b) At resting stage (no stimulus), axolemma is more permeable to potassium ions, very less permeable (nearly impermeable) to sodium ions and impermeable to negatively charged protein. That causes the formation of concentration gradient across axolemma and maintained by sodium-potassium pump. This state is in ***polarised*** state.
c) When stimulus arises, influx of Na+ ions takes place at site A of axollemma (due to opening of voltage gated Na+ channel) and membrane become ***depolarised*** in site A. That creates electrical potential difference across membrane at site A called as action potential. While at site B, positive charge at outer side. So current develop and flow from site A to site B in axoplasm and current flow from site B to A at outside the membrane. So polarity becomes reversed.

d) The depolarised state is followed by efflux of K+ ions take place (due to opening of voltage gated K+ channel and closing of voltage gated Na+ channel) and membrane become ***repolarised***.
e) Sodium potassium pump helps in active transport of ions i.e. transportation of 3 Na+ outwards and 2 K+ inwards. Then the membrane attains polarised state and the potential difference is called as ***resting potential***.

GOLDEN BOX-1

What is the polarisation state of a nerve fibre?

Polarised state of membrane is not conducting nerve impulse and the potential of the membrane is about -70mV. Here sodium and potassium pump (Na+/K+ pump) become active

What is the depolarisation state of a nerve fibre?

The reversal of resting potential is called depolarisation. Here voltage gated Na+ channel become open followed by influx of Na+ ion. That leads to depolarisation, where the membrane potential can increase up to +30 mV.

What is chemical synapse and explain its mechanism?

The transmission of nerve impulse from one neuron to another neuron through neurotransmitters across synaptic cleft is called chemical synapses. When nerve impulse reaches at axon terminal, voltage gated Ca2+ channel present in pre-synaptic region become activated and open into it. That causes fusion of synaptic vessels with the membrane of pre-synaptic region and release neurotransmitters into the synaptic cleft region. These neurotransmitters attach to the receptors of postsynaptic membrane and create depolarization in that region.

What is the role of voltage gated Na+ channel in nerve conduction?

When membrane potential of neuron is stimulated and the potential reach the threshold potential (about -55mV) value, then voltage gated Na+ channel become activated and open. That leads to rapid influx of Na+ ions from ECF (extra cellular fluid) to axoplasm and the membrane become depolarised or attain action potential.

Transmission of Impulses through synapses: It is formed by pre-synaptic neuron and post synaptic neuron. It may or may not be separate by a gap called as synaptic cleft.

a) Two types of synapses i.e. electrical synapses and chemical synapses.

b) In electrical synapses, membranes of both pre and post synaptic neurons are in close proximity and always show faster conduction. This is rare in our system.
c) In chemical synapses, membranes of both pre and post synaptic neurons are separated by synaptic cleft filled with fluid. Here neurotransmitters are present in synaptic vesicles of axon terminals and involved in this transmission.
d) When action potential reach to the pre-synaptic region (axon terminal), synaptic vesicles fuse with the membrane and releases neurotransmitters. This neurotransmitters attach to the receptors of post synaptic region and responsible for the formation of new action potential in post synaptic neuron.

CENTRAL NEURAL SYSTEM:

The control system of our body is brain as it is responsible for voluntary movements. Brain controls thermoregulation, hunger, thirst, circardial rhythm, functioning of involuntary organs (lungs, heart, and kidney et.) and body balance. Human brain s protected by skull and meninges are the outer covering of brain.

Meninges are consisting of duramater (outer layer), arachnoid (very thin middle layer) and piamater (inner layer and directly contact with brain tissue). Forebrain, midbrain and hindbrain are the three components of brain *(figure-2)*.

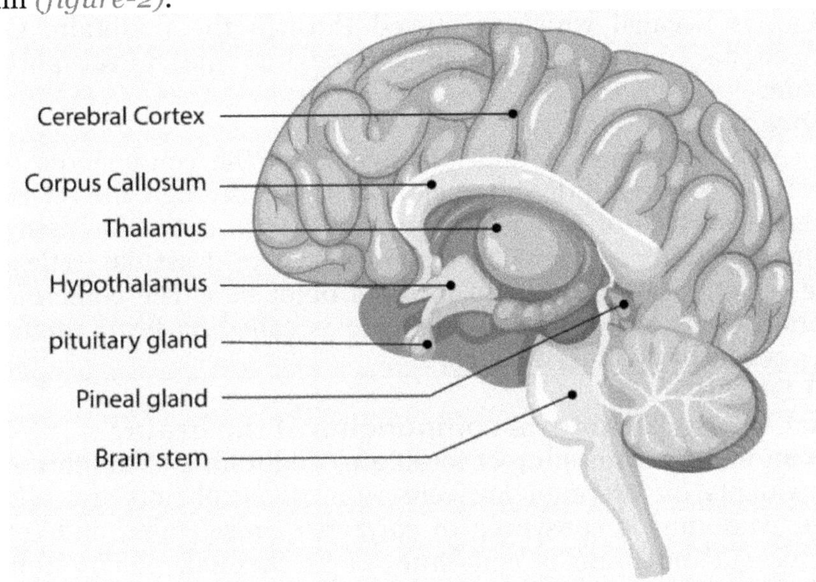

Figure-2: Structure of human brain

Forebrain

Cerebrum (cerebral hemispheres), thalamus and hypothalamus are the components of forebrain. ***Corpus callosum*** (nerve fibres) connects both right and left hemisphere. Cerebral cortex appears grey colour (so called as grey matter and having neural cell bodies) and covers the cerebral hemisphere. ***Association areas*** i.e. motor areas, sensory area and the region neither sensory nor motor are present in cerebral cortex region. These areas are responsible for different functions like communication, memory and intersensory association. Myelinated nerve fibres present at inner part of cerebral hemisphere. So that region appears white and called as white matter.

Thalamus is surrounded by cerebrum and is coordinating centre for both sensory and motor signaling. Hypothalamus presents at the base of thalamus and contains centres for controlling body temperature, urge for drinking and eating. Besides this, hypothalamus contains neurosecretory cells and these cells secrete hypothalamic hormones. ***Limbic system*** (limbic lobes, present at inner part of cerebral hemisphere) is consisting of amygdala, hippocampus etc. This system is involved in regulation of sexual behaviour, expression of emotional reaction (i.e. excitement, pleasure, rage and fear) and motivation.

Midbrain

In between thalamus/hypothalamus, midbrain is present. Cerebral aqueduct is a canal which is passed through the midbrain. Corpora quadrigemina (four round swellings/lobes) is the dorsal portion of midbrain.

Hindbrain

Pons, cerebellum and medulla oblongata are the components of hind brain. Pons connect different region of brain through fibre tract. The convoluted surface of cerebellum provides extra space for many more neurons. Different centres like respiration, cardiovascular reflexes and gastric secretion are present in medulla oblongata. The combination of mid brain, pons and medulla oblongata is called as Brain stem. Brain stem connects brain and spinal cord.

GOLDEN BOX-2

What are the structural components of the brain?

Human brain is consisting of forebrain, midbrain and hindbrain. The components of forebrain are cerebrum, diencephalon and olfactory lobes. Midbrain is consisting of corpora quadrigemina and cerebral peduncle. Hind brain is consisting of cerebellum, pons varolii and medulla oblongata. Mid brain, pons and medulla oblongata are combined and called as brain stem. Brainstem connects brain to spinal cord.

REFLEX ACTION AND REFLEX ARC:

Reflex action is an involuntary process (stimulation of peripheral nervous) in which central nervous system is involved without thought or conscious effort. Withdrawal of body parts when come in contact with extremely hot objects, cold pointed objects or with scary or poisonous animals are the examples of reflex action.

The reflex pathway is consisting of receptor (minimum one afferent neuron) and effector/excitor (one efferent neuron), which are arranged in series.

Sensory organ → afferent neuron → dorsal nerve root → CNS (spinal cord) → efferent neuron → effector (Knee jerk reflex).

DIFFERENCE BETWEEN:

CNS	PNS
1. Central Nervous System 2. It is consisting of brain and spinal cord. 3. Both voluntary and involuntary functions take place. 4. It is enclosed by skull and vertebral column. 5. It is protected by meninges and cerebrospinal fluid.	1. Peripheral Nervous System 2. It is consisting of cranial nerves, spinal nerves, ganglia. 3. It helps in relay of information in from CNS to limbs or organs and vice-versa. 4. It is not enclosed by such bones. 5. No such protection.
Resting potential	**Action potential**
1. It is the potential difference across neural membrane at no stimulus condition. 2. It is about -70 mV. 3. Both Na-K pump and leaky channels maintain this potential. 4. Here Na+ ion is pumped	1. It is the depolarized state or change in membrane potential. 2. It can access potential up to 30 to 40 mV. 3. Stimulus that reaches threshold potential causing action potential. 4. Depolarization is due to

out and K+ ion is pumped in.	influx of Na+ and repolarisation is due to efflux of K+ ion.
Myelinated Axons	**Non-myelinated Axons**
1. It is white in colour due to presence of myelin sheath. 2. These are found in white matter of brain, spinal cord and most peripheral nerves. 3. It shows fast and saltatory nerve conduction.	1. It is grey in colour due to absence of myelin sheath. 2. These are found in grey matter of brain, spinal cord and autonomic nerves. 3. It shows slow and continuous nerve conduction.
Thalamus	**Hypothalamus**
1. Thalamus relays the signals towards cerebral cortex. 2. Thalamus is present above hypothalamus and connects with cerebral cortex.	1. Hypothalamus regulates body temperatures, thirst, hunger etc. 2. Hypothalamus is present at the base of diencephalon and connects with pituitary gland.
Thalamus	**Hypothalamus**
3. Thalamus relays the signals towards cerebral cortex. 4. Thalamus is present above hypothalamus and connects with cerebral cortex.	3. Hypothalamus regulates body temperatures, thirst, hunger etc. 4. Hypothalamus is present at the base of diencephalon and connects with pituitary gland.
Cerebrum	**Cerebellum**
1. Cerebrum is the part of fore brain. It is present at upper part of brain and occupy 2/3rd portion of brain. 2. It is consisting of two	1. Cerebellum is the part of hind brain, which is present below cerebrum. 2. Cerebellum is consisting of two highly folded cerebellar hemispheres.

cerebral hemispheres and each hemisphere is consisting of four lobes. 3. Different voluntary actions, memory, sensory perceptions etc. are controlled by cerebrum.	3. Equilibrium of an organisms body is controlled by cerebellum.
Afferent (Sensory) Neurons	**Efferent (Motor) Neurons**
1. This type of neurons carries impulses towards CNS from sensory receptors. 2. These neurons are present at dorsal root of reflex arc.	1. This type of neurons carries impulses towards effector organs from CNS. 2. These neurons are located in ventral root of reflex arc.
Myeliated nerve fibre	**Non Myelinated nerve fibre**
1. This nerve fibre is covered with myelin sheath. So it appears white. 2. Here, saltatory conduction takes place. That show fast nerve conduction.	1. This nerve fibre is not covered with myelin sheath. So it appears grey. 2. No saltatory conduction that show slow nerve conduction.
Cranial Nerves	**Spinal Nerves**
1. These nerves arise from brain. 2. These nerves are sensory or motor or mixed types. 3. There are 12 pairs of cranial nerves.	1. These nerves arise from spinal cord. 2. These nerves are mixed types 3. There are 31 pairs of cranial nerves.

KNOWLEDGE POINTS:

a) ***Axon hillock*** is the cone shaped elevation part at cell body of nerve cell. Initial segment is the part of axon which is close to axon hillock. Trigger zone is present at the junction in between axon hillock and initial segment.

b) ***Neuroglia*** (smaller than neurons) donot generate action potential. But it can multiply in mature nervous system. In Central Nervous System (CNS), four types of neuroglia are present i.e. astrocytes, oligodendrocytes, microglia and ependymal cells. In Peripheral Nervous System (PNS), two types of neuroglia are presents i.e. Schwann cells and satellite cells.

c) ***Astrocytes*** are in contact with blood capillaries, neurons, pia mater of CNS. These cells create blood brain barrier.

d) ***Oligodendrocytes*** help in formation and maintenance of myelin sheath in CNS.

e) ***Microglial cells*** are phagocytic in nature and phagocytize microbes and damaged nervous tissue.

f) ***Ependymal cells*** are cuboidal or columnar cells (containing microvilli and cilia) and lined the ventricles of brain and spinal cord. These cells help in circulation of cerebrospinal fluids (CSF).

g) ***Satellite cells*** provide structural support to cell bodies of nerve cells and also regulate the exchange of materials in between neural cell bodies and interstitial fluids.

h) ***Schwann cells*** produce myelin sheath in PNS. Schwann cells can enclose 20 or more unmyelinated axons.

i) ***Multiple sclerosis*** is an autoimmune disorder in which there is progressive destruction of myelin sheath in CNS. It is most common in white people and rare in Asians.

j) ***Sciatica*** is caused due to injury in sciatic nerves. The sciatic nerve is the longest nerve in human body and its irritation causes back pain.

k) Inflammation of meninges due to bacterial infection is called ***Meningitis***. If particular region lose its sensation due to anesthetic injection is called as nerve block. Inflammation of nerves is called Neuritis.

l) Due to blood brain barriers, certain substances (like lipid soluble substances, steroid hormones, alcohol, barbiturates, nicotine, caffeine, O_2 and CO_2 gases) are entered into brain tissue from blood , while other substances are prevented.

m) ***CSF*** (cerebrospinal fluid) is consisting of water and small amount of oxygen, glucose , proteins, urea, cations (Na^+, K^+, Ca^{2+}, Mg^+) and anions (Cl^- and HCO_3^-). In adult its volume is about 80 to 105ml. This fluid is circulating in between ventricles of brain, cavities of spinal cord and subarchnoid space.

MULTIPLE CHOICE QUESTIONS (MCQs)-1

1. A person entering an empty room suddenly finds a snake right in front of the opening of door. Which one of the following is likely to happen in his neuro-hormonal control system?
   (a) Sympathetic nervous system is activated releasing epinephrine and norepinephrine from adrenal medulla.
   (b) Neurotransmitters diffuse rapidly across the cleft and transmit a nerve impulse.
   (c) Hypothalamus activates the parasympathetic division of brain.
   (d) Sympathetic nervous system is activated releasing epinephrine and the system is activated releasing epinephrine and norepinephrine from adrenal cortex.
2. If Injury takes place in hypothalamus, that likely to be disrupt the.
   (a) Short-term memory.
   (b) Coordination during locomotion.
   (c) Executive functions, such as decision making.
   (d) Regulation of body temperature
3. The potential difference across resting membrane is negatively charged. This is due to differential distribution of the following ions.
   (a) Na+ and K+ ions
   (b) CO3++ and Cl- ions
   (c) Ca+ + and Mg+ + ions
   (d) Ca+ + and Cl- ions
4. Resting membrane potential is maintained by
   (a) Hormones
   (b) Neurotransmitters
   (c) Ion pumps
   (d) None of these
5. The function of our visceral organs is controlled by
   (a) Sympathetic and somatic neural system.
   (b) Sympathetic and parasympathetic neural system.
   (c) Central and somatic nervous system.
   (d) None of these
6. Which of the following is not involved in knee-jerk reflex?
   (a) Muscle spindle
   (b) Motor neuron

(c) Brain
(d) Inter-neurons

7. Strong emotion is associated with _____ area of brain.
   (a) Cerebral cortex
   (b) Cerebellum
   (c) Limbic system
   (d) Medulla
8. Depolarization occurs due to
   (a) Influx of Na+ (b) Eflux of Na+
   (c) Influx of K+ (c) Eflux of K+
9. The correct sequence for depolarization and repolarization is
   (A) Stimulus applied at a site on polarized membrane.
   (B) Increase the permeability for Na+.
   (C) Generation of A.P. (Action Potential).
   (D) Increase the permeability for K+.
   (E) Restoration of membrane potential
   (a) A → B → C → D → E
   (b) B → A → C → D → E
   (c) A → D → C → B → E
   (d) A → B → D → C → E
10. Unidirectional transmission of the nerve impulse is maintained by
    (a) Interneurons (b) Myelin sheath
    (c) Synapse (d) Membrane polarity
11. Select the total number of true statements from the following.
    I. There are two types of synapses, namely electrical synapses and chemical synapses.
    II. Electrical synapses are rare in our system.
    III. At chemical synapse, the membranes of pre- and post-synaptic neuron are in very close proximity.
    IV. Transmission of an impulse across electrical synapses is very similar to impulse conduction along a single axon.
    V. At a chemical synapse, the membrane of the pre- and post-synaptic neurons is separated by a fluid-filled space called synaptic cleft.
    (a) 2 (b) 3 (c) 4 (d) 5

ASSERTION AND REASON QUESTIONS:

Read the **assertion** *and* **reason** *carefully to mark the correct option out of the options given below:*

(a) If both the assertion and the reason are true and the reason is a correct explanation of the assertion.

(b) If both the assertion and reason are true but the reason is not a correct explanation of the assertion.
(c) If the assertion is true but the reason is false.
(d) If both the assertion and reason are false.

1. **Assertion:** In resting membrane of nerve fibre, ionic gradient is present.
   Reason: ionic gradient is due to sodium and potassium pump.
2. **Assertion:** Thermostat of our body is hypothalamus.
   Reason: Hypothalamus contain centre for body temperature regulation.
3. **Assertion:** Both grey and white matter is present in Spinal cord.
   Reason: Grey matter is the central part of spinal canal.
4. **Assertion:** All efferent neurons are considered as motor neurons.
   Reason: Efferent neurons help in transmission of nerve impulses from the spinal cord to the brain.
5. **Assertion:** Neurotransmitters are the chemicals, which are stored in the synaptic vesicles.
   Reason: These chemicals are released into synaptic cleft from from synaptic vesicles.
6. **Assertion:** Vomiting, coughing and sneezing are the reflex actions; which are developed by Medulla oblongata.
   Reason: These autonomic reflexes are developed by many nerve cells of medulla oblongata.
7. **Assertion:** Neurotransmitters help in transmission of the nerve impulse across a synapse.
   Reason: In synapses, transmission requires neurotransmitters due to presence of synaptic cleft.
8. **Assertion:** In synapses, nerve impulse cannot be transmitted from dendrite or cell body of one neuron to the axon of the next neuron.
   Reason: Synaptic delay occurs at each synapse.
9. **Assertion:** When sound waves are received by ear, the nerve impulse passes auditory nerves towards brain.
   Reason: Through afferent neurons, nerve impulses transmitted from the body organ to the brain.
10. **Assertion:** In neuromuscular junction, motor neuron terminates on a motor end plate.
    Reason: In Motor endplate, receptors detect the changes in the muscle fibre.

***

Chapter-8: CHEMICAL COORDINATION AND INTEGRATION

- **Introduction**
- **Human endocrine system**
- **Mechanism of hormonal action**
- **Golden box**
- **Knowledge points**
- **Multiple choice questions (MCQs)**
- **Assertion & Reason questions**

INTRODUCTION:

All cells of our body are not connected with nerve fibre. So, special type of coordination and integration (i.e. hormones) is required for continuous regulation of cellular functions. The physiological function of the body is regulated by both neural system (fast and short lived) and endocrine system.

- The secretion of endocrine glands (ductless glands) is called as hormones. Hormones (non nutrient chemicals) act as inter cellular messengers, which are produced in trace amount and released into blood.
- Very simple type of endocrine system is present in invertebrates, which produces few hormones.
- In vertebrates, large numbers of hormones are involved in co-ordination.

GOLDEN BOX-1

What is hormone? How exocrine gland is different from endocrine gland?

Hormones are chemical messengers and transfer into target organs/tissue. It influences metabolism, growth and reproduction.

The gland in which secretion takes place through ducts is called as exocrine gland. The secretion can be enzymatic (digestive glands), mucus (mucus glands), and sweat (sweat gland) etc. The gland in which secretion takes place without ducts is called as endocrine gland. The secretion is hormonal (chemical messengers). Pituitary gland, adrenal gland etc. are examples of it.

HUMAN ENDOCRINE SYSTEM:

Human endocrine system is consisting of pituitary, pineal, thyroid, adrenal, pancreas, parathyroid, thymus and gonads (testis/ovary), which are considered as organized endocrine bodies. Besides this, organs like liver, kidney, heart, gastrointestinal tract are also producing hormones.

The Hypothalamus

The basal part of diencephalon is the hypothalamus, which contains neurosecretory cells (nuclei). Two types of hormones are released from these cells i.e. releasing hormone and inhibiting hormone. These hormones regulate pituitary gland by stimulating or inhibiting the secretion of pituitary hormones. Here releasing hormones reach to anterior pituitary gland (adeno-hypophysis) through hypophysisial portal system. While posterior part of pituitary gland (neurohypophysis) is under neural regulation from hypothalamus.

a) GnRH (Gonaotropin releasing hormones) stimulates adeno-hypophysis to produce gonadotrophin (FSH and LH).
b) Somatostatin inhibits the release of growth hormone from adeno-hypophysis.

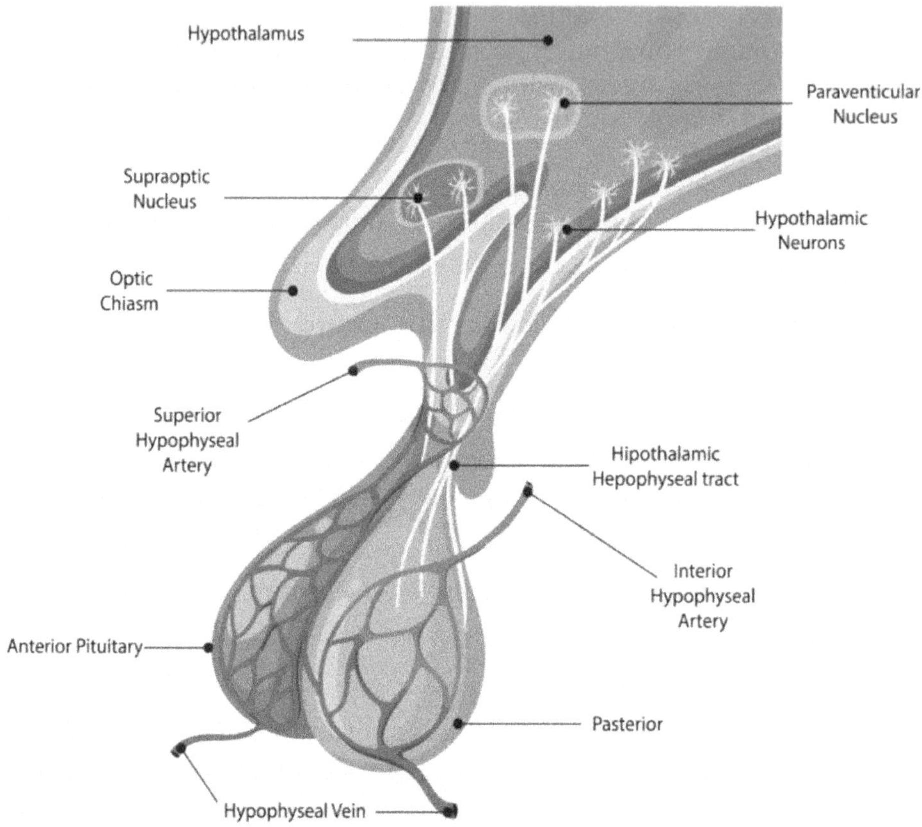

Figure-1: Pituitary gland

The Pituitary Gland:
Sella tursica is the bony cavity, which contains pituitary gland *(figure-1)* and attached to hypothalamus by stalk. Adenohypophysis (pars distalis and pars intermedia) and neurohypophysis (Pars nervosa) are two parts of pituitary gland.

a) Hormones like GH (growth hormones), TSH (thyroid stimulating hormone), PRL (prolactin), FSH (Follicle stimulating hormone), LH (luteinzing hormone), ACTH (adrenocorticotropic hormones are produced from pars distalis. In human, MSH (melanocyte stiulating hormone) is produced from pars distalis as pars intermedia is merged with pars distalis.
b) Hormones like ADH (vasopressin) and oxytocin are synthesized from hypothalamus and axonally transported to Pars nervosa.
c) ***Gigantism*** occurs due to hyper-secretion of GH and responsible for abnormal body growth. ***Dwarfism*** is due to hyposecretion of GH and causes stunted growth.

The growth of mammary glands and formation of milk depend upon prolactin hormone. Glucocorticoids (steroid hormones) synthesize and secreted from adrenal cortex after the influence of ACTH.

Both FSH and LH are ***gonadotropins***. In male, androgen hormone is produced from testis after the influence of LH hormone. Both androgen and FSH regulate spermatogenesis. In female, FSH hormone causes growth and development of ovarian follicle and LH hormone causes ovulation. Again corpus luteum is produced from graafian follicle (mature follicle) after ovulation.MSH regulate the pigmentation of skin after inducing melanocytes.

Oxytocin hormone is responsible for uterine contraction (during parturition) and also helps in milk ejection from mammary glands. While ADH (antidiuretic hormone)/Vasopressin hormone prevent diuresis (loss of water reduced through urine) by resorption of electrolytes and water in distal tubules.

Pineal gland:

Pineal gland is present at the dorsal side of forebrain and secrete melatonin hormone. This hormone is involved in regulation of diurnal rhythm (sleep wake cycle, temperature) of our body and also influences the metabolism, pigmentation, menstrual cycle and defense capability.

Thyroid gland:

Thyroid gland *(figure-2)* is consisting of two lobes. These two lobes are present on either side of trachea and interconnected by isthmus (flap of connective tissue). Each lobe composed of follicles and stromal tissues.

a) Both T4 (tetraiodothyronine/ thyroxine) and T3 (triiodothyronine) hormones are produced from follicular cells. So thyroid

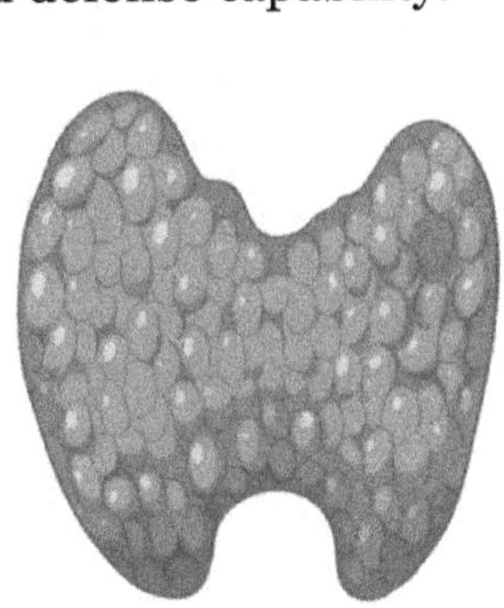

Figure-2: Thyroid gland

gland needs iodine for the normal synthesis of thyroid hormones.Thyroid hormones regulate BMR, help red blood cells formation, helps in maintenance of water and electrolyte balance and control the metabolism of carbohydrate,, proteins and fats.

b) Another hormone i.e. thyrocalcitonin (TCT) is also produced from parafollicular cells of thyroid gland, which helps in regulation blood calcium level.
c) Both ***Hypothyroidism*** and ***Goitre*** (enlargement of thyroid gland) occurs due to deficiency of iodine in the diet.
d) ***Hyperthyroidism*** occurs due to nodules development in thyroid gland or cancer of thyroid gland.
e) ***Cretinism*** shows the characteristics of low intelligence quotient, abnormal skin, mental retardation, deaf mutism etc. It occurs due to hypothyroidism during pregnancy. Cretinism is the stunted growth of growing baby.
f) Again irregular menstrual cycle may occurs in adult female during hypothyroidism. Our body physiology is adversely affected by hyperthyroidism.

Parathyroid Gland *(figure-3)*:
Parathyroid glands are four in numbers; which are present on back side of thyroid gland and secrete peptide hormones called as parathyroid hormone (PTH). Two parathyroid glands are present in each lobe of thyroid gland.

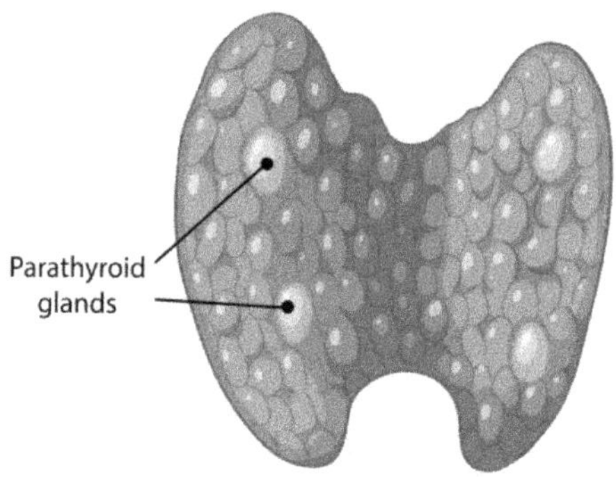

Figure-3: Parathyroid glands

a) PTH causes bone resorption (dissolution/demineralisation) and responsible for increase in calcium level in the blood.
b) Again, PTH (hypercalcemic hormones) also helps in reabsorption of calcium from renal tubules and absorption of calcium from digested food.
c) PTH is antagonistic to TCT.

Thymus:
This gland produces peptide hormones called as ***thymosin*** and helps in the development of immune system i.e. both cell mediated (T lymphocytes) and humoral mediated immunity (antibodies). This gland is present behind sternum, ventral side of aorta and located in between

lungs. At old age, this gland becomes degenerated followed by decrease in level of thymosin. That causes weakening of immune response in old persons.

GOLDEN BOX-2:

Write the name of disorders that occurs due to hormonal deficiency

- The deficiency of insulin causes ***diabetes mellitus***, where the level of glucose decreases in blood
- ***Goitre*** occurs due to the deficiency of thyroxine hormone, where swelling of thyroid gland takes place
- ***Cretinism*** occurs in infants due to the deficiency of thyroxine hormone, where stunted growth and mental retardation appears

Adrenal gland:

Adrenal gland present at anterior side of kidney and consisting of outer cortex region (produce corticoids hormone) and inner medulla region (produce catecholamines hormones).

Corticoid hormones are Mineralocoticoids, glucocorticoids and small amount of androgenic steroids.

a) Mineralocorticoids (mainly ***Aldosterone***) regulate water and electrolyte balance in our body, body fluid volume, osmotic pressure and phosphate ions. Aldosterone stimulates reabsorption of Na+ and water and excretion of K+ and phosphate ions.
b) Glucocorticoids (mainly ***cortisol***) stimulate gluconeogenesis, proteolysis, lipolysis and inhibit aminoacid utilization and cellular uptake. Cortisol stimulates erythropoiesis, suppress immune response and produce anti-inflammatory reaction.
c) Androgenic steroids help in growth of axial hair, pubic hair and facial hair at puberty.

Catecholamines are adrenaline and noradrenaline (emergency hormone or hormones for fight/flight). These two hormones are produced during emergency condition.

i. These emergency hormone increases heart beat, heart strength contraction, rate of respiration, alertness, sweating.
ii. Besides this, it is responsible for pilo-erection (raising of hairs) and dilation of pupil.

Pancreas

This composite gland is both exocrine and endocrine in function. Its endocrine parts are islets of Langerhans (1 to 2 million), which are representing 1 to 2% of normal human pancreas. The remaining percentages are known as pancreatic acini (release pancreatic juice).

a) Both α-cells and β-cells are main cells of islets of Langerhans and release peptide hormones i.e. glucagon and insulin respectively.
b) Glucagon hormone (acts on hepatocytes) maintains blood sugar level and increases blood sugar level (hyperglycemia) through glycogenolysis and gluconeogenesis. Besides, this hormone reduces cellular uptake of glucose and its utilization. So this hormone is also called as ***hyperglycemic hormone***.
c) Insulin hormone (acts on hepatocytes and adipocytes) regulate glucose level and decrease blood glucose level (hypoglycemia) through glycogenesis.
d) Both glucagon and insulin maintain glucose homeostasis. Diabetes mellitus can be caused due to prolonged hyperglycemia. D. mellitus is associatd with loss of glucose through urine and ketone bodies formation.This can be treated with insulin therapy.

Testis

In male, testis (one pair) is considered as primary sex organ and endocrine gland, which is present outside abdomen (within scrotal sac). Seminiferous tubules, stroma or interstitial tissue and leydig cells (interstitial tissue) are the components of testis. Androgen (testosterone) hormone is produced from leydig cells.

a) This hormone regulates the development, maturation and functions of male accessory organs (epididymis, vas deferens, seminal vesicles, prostate gland, urethra etc.
b) This hormone is responsible for muscular growth, facial growth, axillary hair growth, aggressiveness, low pitch voice etc.
c) ***Androgens*** are also responsible for stimulation of spermatogenesis, influence on male sexual behaviour (libido) and anabolic effects on metabolism (both protein and carbohydrates).

Ovary

In female, one pair of ovaries is considered as primary sex organ (produce one ovum during each menstrual cycle) and endocrine gland. Ovarian follicles and stromal tissue are the components of ovary. Estrogen and progesterone are the steroid hormones which are produced from ovary.

- Growing ovarian follicles help in synthesis and release estrogen hormone.

- This ***estrogen*** hormone is responsible for development of growing ovarian follicles, growth and activities of secondary sex organs in female, secondary sexual characters in female (high pitch voice) and mammary gland development.
- Pregnancy is supported by ***progesterone*** hormone. This hormone helps in formation of alveoli of mammary gland and milk secretion.

Other hormones

a) **ANF** (Atrial natriuretic factor)**:** This is peptide hormone which is produced from atrial wall of heart and responsible for dilation of blood vessel. In this way, blood pressure decreases.
b) **Erythropoietin:** It is also peptide hormone which is produced from JG (Juxta glomerular) cells of kidney and responsible for RBC formation i.e. erythropoiesis.
c) **Gastrin:** This hormone is responsible for secretion of HCL and pepsinogen from gastric glands of gastrointestinal tract.
d) **Secretin:** This hormone causes secretion of water and bicarbonate ions from exocrine part of pancreas.
e) **CCK** (cholecystokinin)**:** This hormone causes pancreatic enzymes and bile from pancreas and gall bladder respectively.
f) **GIP** (gastric inhibitory peptide): Gastric secretion and motility are inhibited by this hormone.
g) **Growth factors:** These hormones are produced from other endocrine tissue and responsible for normal growth of tissue and repairing/regeneration

MECHANISM OF HORMONE ACTION:

The receptors for hormone can be membrane bound receptors (present on the cell membrane of target cells) and intracellular receptors (present inside the target cell). Most intracellular receptors are nuclear receptors. These receptors are specific (each receptor is specific to one hormone). Hormone-receptor complex causes biochemical changes (changes in physiology and metabolism) in target tissue.

a) Cyclic AMP, IP3, Ca++ etc. are ***second messengers***, which are produced from target cell due to interaction of hormone and membrane bound receptor. Here hormones do not enter into target cell.
b) Hormones like steroid hormone, iodothyronine etc. mostly regulate gene expression or chromosomal function after interacting with intra-cellular receptors. Here, there is interaction

in between hormone receptor complex and genome of target cell. That causes physiological and developmental effects.

Hormones are categorized into four major types on the basis of its chemical nature i.e.

- Amino-acid derivatives (Epinephrine)
- Peptide, polypeptide, protein hormones (insulin, glucagon, pituitary hormone, hypothalamic hormone etc.)
- Iodo-thyronines (thyroid hormones)
- Steroids (Cortisol, testosterone, estradiol and progesterone)

Hormones	Functions
(a) Parathyroid hormone (PTH)	This hormone is secreted from parathyroid glands. It causes bone resorption, activation of vitamin D, calcium reabsorption in kidney and calcium reabsorption in intestine. In this way, this hormone causes increase in the level of calcium ions in blood.
(b) Thyroid hormones (T3 & T4)	These hormones are produced from thyroid gland and helps in growth, development, metabolic activity by regulating metabolism. Besides this, this hormone also regulates body temperature.
(c) Thymosins	It is secreted from thymus gland and helps in maturation of T-lymphocytes; which later differentiate into different types of T cells.
(d) Androgens	It is secreted from testes and responsible for secondary sexual characters and bone density in male.
(e) Estrogens	It is secreted from ovaries and responsible for female secondary sexual characters and maintenance of pregnancy. Besides this, this hormones help in bone health.
(f) Insulin and glucagon	Insulin hormone is produced by β-cells of islets of langerhans and maintains sugar level in blood by converting extra glucose to glycogen. Glucagon hormone is produced from α-cells of islets of langerhans and convert glycogen to glucose.

Hormones	Functions
Hyperglycemic and hypoglycemic hormone	In *hyperglycemic hormone*, blood glucose level increases (e.g. growth hormone, glucagon, cortisol, and epinephrine). In *hypoglycemic hormone*, blood glucose level decreases (e.g. Insulin).
Hypercalcemic hormone	In this hormone, the level of calcium ions increases in blood (e.g. parathyroid hormone i.e. PTH.
Gonardotrophic hormones	These hormones (LH & FSH) are released from adenohypophysis and stimulate gonards (Testes and ovary). In female, LH induces ovulation and FSH helps in maturation of ovarian follicles. In male, LH induces the release of testosterone and FSH helps in spermatogenesis.
Progesterone hormone	**These hormones** are released from corpus luteum of ovary. This hormone helps in maintenance of endometrium for implantation purposes.
Atrial natriuretic factor	Blood pressure lowering hormone is the **atrial natriuretic factor** (ANF). This hormone acts as vasodilator.
Androgen and Estrogen	Andogen is the male sex hormones, which are produced from testis; while estrogen is the female sex hormone produced from ovaries.

DIFFERENCE BETWEEN:

Adenohypophysis	Neurohypophysis
1. It is consisting of glandular cells.	1. It is consisting of nerve fibres and pituicytes.
2. It is connected to hypothalamus indirectly	2. It is connected to hypothalamus directly

through hypothalamo-hypophyseal portal system. 3. It is controlled by hormones (i.e. both releasing and inhibiting hormones) released from hypothalamus 4. Hormones like GH, ACTH, GTH, PRL, TSH etc. are released from this region.	through nerve fibres. 3. It is controlled by nerve impulses released from hypothalamus. 4. Hormones like Oxytocin, ADH are released from this region.

KNOWLEDGE POINTS:

- Most hormones first enter into interstitial fluid followed by blood stream. Both hormones and neurotransmitters are bind to the receptors of target cells. Chemicals like norepinephrine released as hormones from adrenal medulla region and as a neurotransmitters from sympathetic ganglions neurons.
- Amine hormones, peptide and protein hormones and eicosanoid hormones are ***water soluble hormones***. Catecholamines (epinephrine, norepinephrine and dopamine), histamine, serotonin and melatonin are amine hormones. ADH and oxytocin are peptide hormones. Insulin is protein hormones. Prostaglandin (local hormones is eicosanoid hormones).
- Steroid hormones and thyroid hormones (T3 and T4) are ***lipid soluble hormones***. Steroid hormones are derived from cholesterol. Thyroid hormones are synthesized by attaching iodine with tyrosine amino acids.
- ***Addisons disease*** is caused due to hyposecretion of glucocorticoids and aldosterone. The symptoms of this disease are weight loss, hypoglycemia, nausea, mental lethargy etc.
- If more amount of estrogen is formed in male due to tumor in adrenal gland. That leads to development of mammary gland

and called as ***Gynacomastia.***

- If more amount of androgen is produced in female due to tumor in adrenal gland. Then that causes ***virilism***.

MULTIPLE CHOICE QUESTIONS (MCQs)-1:

1. A hypothalamic hormone, GnRH, needed in reproduction, acts on
   (a) The anterior pituitary gland and stimulates the secretion of LH and oxytocin
   (b) Posterior pituitary gland and stimulates the secretion of LH and relaxin
   (c) Posterior pituitary gland and stimulates the secretion of oxytocin and FSH
   (d) Anterior pituitary gland and stimulates the secretion of LH and FSH.
2. Hypersecretion of growth hormone in adults does not cause further increase in height, because
   (a) Growth hormone becomes inactive in adults
   (b) Muscle fiber does not grow in size after birth
   (c) Bones lose their sensitivity to growth hormones in adults
   (d) Epiphyseal plates close after adolescence
3. Name a peptide hormone which acts mainly on hepatocytes, adipocytes and enhances cellular glucose uptake and utilization
   (a) Gastrin
   (b) Insulin
   (c) Secretin
   (d) Glucagon
4. Find out temporary endocrine gland in the human body from followings.
   (a) Pineal gland
   (b) Corpus luteum
   (c) Corpus allatum
   (d) Corpus cardiacum
5. The posterior pituitary gland is not a "true" endocrine gland because
   (a) It only stores and releases hormones
   (b) It is provided with a duct
   (c) It secretes enzymes
   (d) It is under the regulation of the hypothalamus
6. Select pair of hormones, which are not antagonistic to each other

(a) Relaxin – Inhibin
(b) Insulin – Glucagon
(c) Parathormone – Calcitonin
(d) Aldosterone – Atrial Natriuretic Factor

7. Which hormone is not involved in sugar metabolism?
(a) Glucagon
(b) Insulin
(c) Cortisone
(d) Aldosterone

8. Which hormone is synthesized elsewhere and stored, but released by the master gland
(a) Luteinizing hormone
(b) Antidiuretic hormone
(c) Prolactin
(d) Melanocyte stimulating hormone

9. Fight-or-flight reactions cause activation of
(a) the pancreas leading to a reduction in the blood sugar levels
(b) the adrenal medulla, leading to increased secretion of epinephrine and norepinephrine
(c) the kidney, leading to suppression of the renin-angiotensin-aldosterone pathway
(d) the parathyroid glands, leading to increased metabolic rate

10. A pregnant female delivers a baby who suffers from stunted growth, mental retardation, low intelligence quotient and abnormal skin. This is the result of
(a) deficiency of iodine in the diet
(b) oversecretion of pars distalis
(c) low secretion of growth hormone
(d) cancer of the thyroid gland.

MULTIPLE CHOICE QUESTIONS (MCQs)-2:

1. Name a peptide hormone which acts mainly on hepatocytes, adipocytes and enhances cellular glucose uptake and utilization.
(a) Glucagon
(b) Secretion
(c) Gastrin
(d) Insulin

2. Osteoporosis, an age-related disease of skeletal system, may occur due to
(a) High concentration of Ca^{++} and Na^{+}

(b) Decreased level of estrogen
(c) Accumulation of uric acid leading to inflammation of joints
(d) Immune disorder affecting neuromuscular junction leading to fatigue

3. Match list I (Hormone) with list II (Target) and select the correct answer :-

List - I	List - II
A. ACTH	1. Thyroid
B. Prolactin	2. Adrenal cortex
C. TSH	3. Mammary gland
D. Oxytocin	4. Smooth muscle of uterine wall

(a) A - 1, B - 2, C - 3 & D - 4
(b) A - 2, B - 3, C- 1 & D - 4
(c) A - 2, B - 3, C - 4 & D - 1
(d) A - 3, B - 4, C - 1 & D – 2

4. Changes in GnRH pulse frequency in females is controlled by circulating levels of:
(a) Estrogen and progesterone
(b) Estrogen and inhibin
(c) Progesterone only
(d) Progesterone and inhibin

5. Find the correct statement on 'inhibin':
(a) Inhibits the secretion of LH, FSH and Prolactin
(b) Is produced by granulose cells in ovary and inhibits the secretion of FSH
(c) Is produced by granulose cells in ovary and inhibits the secretion of LH
(d) Is produced by nurse cells in testes and inhibits the secretion of LH

6. Graves' disease is caused due to
(a) Hypersecretion of thyroid gland
(b) Hyporsecretion of adrenal gland
(c) Hypersecretion of adrenal gland
(d) Hyporsecretion of thyroid gland

7. Fight-or-flight reactions can cause the activation of

(a) The parathyroid glands, leading to increased metabolic rate.
(b) The kidney, leading to suppression of rennin-angiotensin-aldosterone pathway.
(c) The adrenal medulla, leading to increased secretion of epinephrine and norepinephrine.
(d) The pancreas leading to a reduction in the blood sugar levels.

8. Consider the following statements.
    A. Calcitonin is non-iodised.
    B. Calcitonin is secreted by parafollicular cells.
    C. Calcitonin regulates the calcium level in blood.
    D. Calcitonin is also called as TCT (Thyrocalcitonin).
    E. TCT is hyperglycemic agent (factor).

    Select the option containing correct statements from the above given statements:-
    (a) A, B and D
    (b) A, B, C and D
    (c) C, D and E
    (d) B, C, D and E
9. A chemical signal that has both endocrine and neural roles is
    (a) Melatonin
    (b) Calcitonin
    (c) Epinephrine
    (d) Cortisol
10. Select correct statement about the hormone action in humans.
    (a) Glucagon is secreted by "cells of islets of Langerhans and stimulates glycogenolysis.
    (b) Secretion of thymosins is stimulated with aging.
    (c) In females, FSH first binds with specific receptors on ovarian cell membrane.
    (d) FHS stimulates the secretion of oestrogen and progesterone.
11. Select correct statement in relation to the endocrine system.
    (a) Adenopophysis is under direct neural regulation of the hypothalamus.
    (b) Organs in the body like gastrointestinal tract, heart, kidney and liver do not produce any hormones.

(c) Non-nutrient chemicals produced by the body in trace amount that act as intercellular messenger are known as hormones.
(d) Releasing and inhibitory hormones are produced by the pituitary gland

12. Life saving hormone of adrenal cortex is not related with :-
    (a) Increase gluconeogenesis
    (b) Increase lipogenesis
    (c) Increase lipolysis, increase erythropoiesis
    (d) Increase protein synthesis
13. If adrenal cortex is injured, then which hormone secretion is not affected?
    (a) Aldosterone
    (b) Both androstenedione and dehydroepiandrosterone
    (c) Adrenaline
    (d) Cortisol
14. Low Ca2+ in the body fluid may be the cause of
    (a) Tetany
    (b) Anaemia
    (c) Angina pectoris
    (d) Gout
15. The toxic agents present in food which interfere with thyroxin synthesis lead to the development of.
    (a) Toxic goitre
    (b) Cretinism
    (c) Simple goitre
    (d) Thyrotoxicosis

ASSERTION AND REASON QUESTIONS:

Read the **assertion** *and* **reason** *carefully to mark the correct option out of the options given below:*

(a) If both the assertion and the reason are true and the reason is a correct explanation of the assertion.
(b) If both the assertion and reason are true but the reason is not a correct explanation of the assertion.
(c) If the assertion is true but the reason is false.
(d) If both the assertion and reason are false.

1. **Assertion:** Hormones are intercellular messengers and nutrient substances.

Reason: Large amount of hormones are generally produced.

2. **Assertion:** The neurohypophysis is under the direct neural contact with hypothalamus.
   Reason: The secretion of hypothalamic neuron comes to neurohypophysis and the release from it.
3. **Assertion:** Gigantism occurs due to hyper secretion of GH.
   Reason: During gigantism, abnormal growth of body takes place.
4. **Assertion:** Blood calcium level is regulated by thyroid gland.
   Reason: Thyrocalcitonin regulates blood calcium level. It is a protein hormone, which is secreted from thyroid gland.
5. **Assertion:** Oxytocin hormone is considered as 'birth hormone'.
   Reason: Oxytocin is responsible for uterine contraction in female during child birth.
6. **Assertion:** The level of calcium ions increases in blood due to PTH.
   Reason: Bone resorption occurs due to PTH.
7. **Assertion:** The posterior pituitary is also called as Neurohypophysis or Pars nervosa.
   Reason: Both oxytocin and vasopressin are stored and release from posterior pitutary gland.
8. **Assertion:** Antidiueretic hormone (ADH) is also known as vasopressin.
   Reason: In distal tubules of nephrons, ADH stimulates the reabsorption of water and electrolyte. In this way, diuresis becomes reduced.
9. **Assertion:** Goitre is the enlargement of thyroid gland.
   Reason: Only the deficiency of iodine causes Goitre.
10. **Assertion:** Weak immune response present in old person.
    Reason: In old person, thymus becomes degenerated.
11. **Assertion:** If adrenal cortex is removed, person cannot be dead.
    Reason: Adrenal cortex is not important for survival of individual.

***

Chapter-9: BIOMOLECULES

- **Introduction**
- **Metabolites**
- **Lipids**
- **Polysachharides**
- **Proteins**
- **Nucleic acids**
- **Enzymes**
- **Golden box**
- **Knowledge points**
- **Multiple choice questions (MCQs)**
- **Assertion & Reason questions**

INTRODUCTION:

In our biosphere, diversity of living organisms is found. These living organisms are consisting of elements and compounds. Carbon, hydrogen, oxygen etc. are the elements present in plant tissue, animal tissue or microbial paste etc. Elements present in earth crust are also present in living tissue, while carbon and hydrogen are higher in living organisms than earth's crust *(Table-1)*.

Elements	% weight of human body	% weight of earth crust
Oxygen (O)	65	46.6
Carbon (C)	18.5	0.03
Hydrogen (H)	9.5	0.14
Nitrogen (N)	3.3	Very little
Calcium (Ca)	1.5	3.6
Sulphur (S)	0.3	0.03
Sodium (Na)	0.2	2.8
Magnesium (Mg)	0.1	2.1
Silicon (Si)	Negligible	27.7
• Adapted from CNR Rao, Understanding chemistry, Universities Press, Hyderabad.		

Table-1: Comparison of elements present in non living and living matter.

Analysis of chemical composition in living tissue:

Living tissue (a vegetable or piece of liver etc.) is grind with trichloroacetic acid (Cl_3CCOOH) with mortar and pestle. In this way, thick slurry is formed. Two types of fraction are formed i.e. filtrate (acid soluble pool) and retentate (acid insoluble fraction). Thousands of organic compounds are found in acid soluble pool.

If the tissue is fully burnt, then all carbon compounds are oxidized into CO_2 and water vapour. The remaining part is called "ash"; which contains inorganic elements *(Table-2)* like calcium, magnesium, sulphate, phosphate etc. Here sulphate and phosphate are acid soluble fraction.

Micromolecles (biomicromolecules):

a) Molecular weights vary from 18 to 800 daltons (Da) approximately. Acid soluble fraction (roughly cytoplasmic composition).
b) Lipids are micromolecules, but they are acid insoluble and found in acid insoluble fraction. Fragments of cell membrane get separated along with insoluble pool.

Macromolecules (biomacromolecules): Molecular weight exceeds 800 daltons (Da) is the acid insoluble fraction.

METABOLITES:Primary metabolites: These metabolites are isolated from living organisms and involved in its growth and development. Besides this, it has role in physiological processes. e.g. amino acids, sugars etc. **Secondary metabolites:** These metabolites are not involved in growth and development. But it helps the organisms in other way. Besides this, some secondary metabolites have ecological importance *(Table-2)*. e.g. alkaloids, flavonoids, rubber, essential oil, antibiotics, coloured pigments, scent, gum, spices.

A		B	
Component	**Formula**	**Pigments**	Carotenoids, Anthocyanin etc.
Sodium	Na^+	**Alkaloids**	Morphine, Codeine, etc.
Potassium	K^+	**Terpenoides**	Monoterpenes,Diterpenes etc.
Magnesium	Mg^{++}	**Essential oils**	Lemon grass oil etc.
Calcium	Ca^{++}	**Toxins**	Abrin, Ricin
Water	H2O	**Lectins**	Concanavaline-A
Compounds	NaCl, $CaCO_3$, PO_4^{3-} ,SO_4^{2-}	**Drugs**	Vinblastin, Curcumin etc.
		Polymeric substances	Rubber, gums, cellulose

Table-2: (A) List of Representative inorganic constituents of living tissues (B) Some Secondary Metabolites

LIPIDS:

Lipids are micro-molecules, water insoluble and could be simple fatty acids. When carboxylic group attach to alkyl or R group (methyl or ethyl or higher number CH2 groups up to 19 carbons) , then it is considered as fatty acid. e.g. Palmitic acid (16 carbons), Arachidonic acid (20 carbons).

a) Fatty acids are categorized into saturated (without double bonds) and unsaturated (with one or more double bonds) types.
b) Glycerol (trihydroxy propane) is simple lipids. Fatty acids are esterifies with glycerol and form many lipids like monoglycerides, diglycerides and triglycerides. On the basis of melting point, these lipids are called fats (high) and oil (low; gingelly oil).
c) Besides this, phosphorous and phosphorylated organic compound are also associated with simple lipid and called as compound lipids (phospholipids, sphingolipids etc.). Phospholipids are found in

cell membrane. E.g. Lecithin. Sphingolipids present in neural tissue.

POLYSACHHARIDES:

They are macromolecules which are consisting of monosaccharides and found in acid insoluble pellet. e.g. Cellulose, starch, glycogen, inulin, chitin etc.

a) Cellulose (present in plant cell wall, paper) is homopolymers and consisting of glucose (monosaccharides)
b) Starch (helical secondary structure) is the store house of energy in plant tissues. Starch *(figure-2)* can hold iodine and give blue colour.
c) Glycogen can also be called as animal starch.
d) Chitin is complex polysaccharides, which is present in exoskeleton of arthropods. But in nature, more complex polysaccharides (mostly homopolymers) are present, which are consisting of amino sugars and chemically modified sugars i.e. glucosamine and N-acetyl glucosamine etc.

GOLDEN BOX-1:

Write about macromolecules with examples.

Macromolecules like carbohydrates (starch, glycogen etc.), proteins (Enzymes, haemoglobin etc.), lipids (Fats, oils, steroids etc.), nucleic acids (DNA, RNA) are the monomers of smaller units. They are complex molecules and essential in all living organisms because these molecules are involved in different biochemical reaction.

Explain tertiary structure of proteins.

The tertiary structure of proteins are stable and important for protein's functions, which are formed due to folding of secondary structure and stabilized by different interactions i.e. hydrogen bonds, disulfide bonds, ionic bonds, hydrophobic interaction etc. and formed 3D shaped of single peptide.

Write down some small molecular weight biomolecules along with their manufacturing industry and buyers.

Glucose, fructose, ribose, cholesterol, lactic acids, glycerol, adenine, guanine, thymine, uracil etc. are small molecular weight biomolecules. These biomolecules are manufactured in different industries like starch industries, chemical, biochemical industries etc. Glucose (simple sugar & monosaccharide), fructose (monosaccharide) and ribose (5-carbon sugar) and other derivatives are required in different in biotech, pharmaceutical and food & beverage companies. Cholesterol (lipid molecule & steroid precursor), Lactic acids and glycerol (component of phospholipids & glycerides) are required in buyers like pharmaceuticals, cosmetics etc. Adenine (purine), guanine (purine), thymine (pyrimidine) and uracil (pyrimidine) are used in pharmaceuticals, biotech, and research labs.

PROTEINS:

Amino acids are organic compounds which contain carboxylic/ acidic group and amino group in α-carbon that means in same carbon. So they are considered as α-amino acids (substituted methane). Here hydrogen, carboxyl group, amino group and R-group (variable group) are the four substituted groups. The R group is different in different amino acids like hydrogen (in glycine), a methyl group (in alanine), hydroxyl methyl (serine) etc.

Based on the numbers of amino or carboxyl groups, amino acids are grouped into three types i.e.

a) Acidic amino acids (2 carboxylic groups and 1 amino group; e.g. glutamic acid)
b) Basic amino acids (2 amino groups and 1 carboxylic group; e.g. lysine)
c) Neutral amino acids (1 amino group and 1 carboxylic group; e.g. valine)

Phenylalanine, tryptophan, tyrosine are the aromatic amino acids. In amino acids, the functional groups ($-NH_2$ and $-COOH$ groups) are ionizable in nature. So the structure of amino acids changes in different solution of pH.

Linear chains of amino acids are linked by peptide bonds and form polypeptide or proteins. Protein is a heteropolymer and not homopolymer. Many functions of living system (transport nutrients across cell membrane, some fight infectious diseases, some are hormones, some are enzymes etc.) are performed by proteins. Twenty types of amino acids.

a) *Essential amino acids*: Essential amino acids are present dietary protein. e.g. Phenyl alanine, Valine, Methionine, Isoleucine, Leucine, Lysine, Tryptophan, Arginine, Histidine, Threonine.
b) *Non essential amino acids*: Glycine, Glutamine, Glutamic acid, Alanine, Aspargine, Aspartic acid, Tyrosine, Serine, proline, cysteine.

Collagen: It is the most abundant proteins in animal world.

RuBisCO: It is the most abundant protein in whole biosphere.

GOLDEN BOX-2:

Write down some list of proteins which are used as therapeutic agents and other uses.

Insulin is the peptide hormone, which is used in type-1 & type-2 diabetes. *Erythropoetin* is the peptide hormone, which is used to treat anemia. ***Interferons*** is the cytokine, which is used to treat cancer, hepatitis etc. *Monoclonal antibodies* are used against cancer, autoimmune diseases. *Blood coagulating factors* like factor-VII & IX, which are used in hemophilia A & B.

Collagen is used in preparation of creams, gels etc. *Keratin* is used in the treatment of damaged hair and skin. *Silk proteins* are used in skin treatment.

Find out the composition of triglyceride.

Triglycerides are the composition of one glycerol and three fatty acids (e.g. animal body fats, vegetables oil).

Can we build biomolecules model physically by using atomic models?

Yes, the model of biomolecules can be made from commercially available ball and stick model kit.

Find out the structure of alanine amino acid.

The formula of alanine amino acid is $CH_3-CH(NH_2)-COOH$

Structure of proteins

In protein, left end amino acid represent 1st amino acid (N-terminal amino acid); while the right end represent last amino acids (C-terminal acid).Only right handed helix (secondary structure) is observed. The folded form of protein chain is the tertiary structure (hollow woolen ball) and gives 3D view. Many biological activities of proteins are due to tertiary structure.

Quaternary structure (cube or plate etc. form) of protein is consisting of more than one polypeptide. Haemoglobin (2α and 2β subunits) is the best example of quaternary structure.

GOLDEN BOX-3:

What is gum and how it is different from Fevicol?

Gum is natural synthetic polymer and used in food for chewing. So it is considered as edible. But fevicol is adhesive substances.

What are the qualitative tests for target biomolecules like proteins, fats and oils and amino acids and explain their results in different samples?

Biuret Test is used for the analysis proteins. Both saliva and sweat show positive results. Both fruit juice and urine shoe negative results.

<u>*Grease Spot Test / Sudan III Staining*</u> are used for analysis of fat and oils. Saliva, sweat, fruit juice and urine show negative results.
<u>*Ninhydrin Test*</u> is used for analysis of amino acids. Saliva, sweat and urine show positive results. Fruit juice usually show negative results

What is the percentage of cellulose in all the plants of biosphere? What is the amount manufactured paper and consumption of plant materials by man annually? What is the loss of vegetation?

Plant biomass is produced due to photosynthesis. Around 40-50% of plants biomass is cellulose, which is about 120 billion metric tons /year. It is estimated that 400 million tons paper are produced per year. So paper consumption per year is about 1/300 th of annual cellulose production.

What are the important properties of enzymes?

- Activation energy of a reaction becomes lower in the presence of enzyme. That causes faster reaction.
- Enzyme work properly in the optimum temperature and pH.
- Enzymes are used repeatedly.
- Specific enzyme catalyzes one type of reaction.
- Activators or inhibitors can regulate the enzyme activity.

NUCLEIC ACIDS:

Heterocyclic rings are found in living organisms. These rings are nitrogenous base (adenine, guanine, cytosine, uracil and thymine), sugars. ***Nucleosides*** (Adenosine, Guanosine, thymidine, uridine and thymidine) are the combination of nitrogenous base and sugar. ***Nucleotides*** (Adenylic acids, thymidylic acids , guanylic acids, uridylic acids and cytidylic acids) are the combination of nucleosides and phosphoric acids.

DNA and ***RNA*** are the nucleic acids consisting of nucleotides and functions as genetic materials. Nucleic acids (macromolecules) are polynucleotides; which form true molecular fraction with polysaccharides and polypeptides.

The components of nucleotide is

a) Heterocyclic compound or nitrogenous bases (i.e. adenine, guanine, uracil, cytosine and thymine). Purine (adenine and guanine), Pyrimidine (uracil, cytosine, thymine)
b) Monosaccharide i.e. ribose for RNA or 2' deoxyribose for DNA

Phosphoric acid or phosphate

ENZYMES:

Enzyme catalyses the biochemical reaction and it is differ from inorganic catalyst. At high temperature (>40°C), enzymes become damaged while inorganic catalyst works efficiently. But certain enzymes which are separated from thermophilic organisms (live under extremely high temperature) are stable at 80° to 90°C. Some nucleic acids are enzymes like ***ribozymes***.

Like protein, enzymes have primary, secondary and tertiary structure. The *active site is present in its tertiary structure*, where substrate attached.

Chemical Reactions:

The amount of products formed per unit time is the rate of a physical or chemical process. Temperature and other factors affect the rates of physical and chemical processes. Hydrolysis of starch into glucose is *organic chemical reaction.* $Ba(OH)_2 + H_2SO_4 \rightarrow BaSO_4 + 2H_2O$ is an *inorganic chemical reaction.*

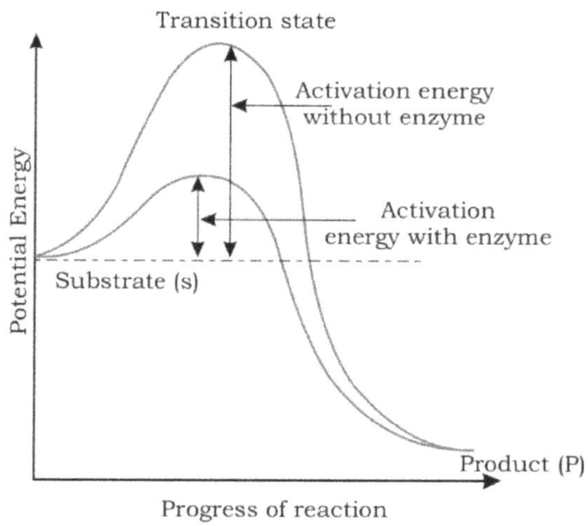

Figure-1: Activation energy in rate of reaction

The rate of reaction becomes double or reduced to half in every 10°C change in either direction. The catalyzing rate becomes vast higher than un-catalyzing rate.

In the absence of enzyme (carbonic anhydrase), *200 molecules of H_2CO_3 are formed in an hour*; while in the presence of enzymes, *6 lakh molecules of H_2CO_3 are formed per second.* That means the reaction rate becomes increased 10 million times and activation energy decrease in the presence of enzymes *(figure-1)*.

Thousands types of enzymes are known and each enzyme has unique catalyzing power. In metabolic pathway, same enzyme complex or different enzymes are involved like glycolysis process, anaerobic respiration in skeletal muscle etc.

E + S → ES complex (transient) → E + P.

Y axis represents potential energy; while X-axis represents structural transformation or state through transient state.

Nature of enzyme action

Steps for catalytic cycle of an enzyme are as follows.

a) Binding of substrate to the active site of enzyme
b) The shape of enzyme becomes altered and fitting more tightly around substrate.
c) Breaking of chemical bonds in substrate and form enzyme-product complex. Then products become released and enzyme is free to bind another molecule.

Factors affecting enzyme activity

Factors like temperature, pH, change in substrate concentration, certain chemicals (inhibitors) can affect enzyme activity.

(i) Each enzyme becomes more active at its optimum temperature and pH. At low temperature, enzyme becomes temporarily inactive. But at high temperature, enzyme becomes denatured.
(ii) The enzymatic reaction increased first with increase in substrate concentration. When the activity reached at maximum velocity (Vmax), then there is no further increase in activity.
(iii)Inhibitors, which are similar with substrate (on the basis of molecular weight) compete with substrate for the active site of enzyme and inhibit enzyme activity. They are called as competitive inhibitors. e.g. malonate compete with succinate and inhibits succinic dehydrogenase (used to control bacterial pathogens)

Enzyme classification

There are 6 classes of enzymes and each class has 4-13 subclasses.

a) Oxidoreductase/ dehydrogenase → both oxidation and reduction in two substrate. e.g., S reduced + S' oxidised → S oxidised + S' reduced.
b) Transferase → Transfer of a group between a pair of substrate. E.g. S - G + S' → S + S' – G
c) Hydrolases → responsible for hydrolysis of different bonds like ester, ether, peptide, glycosidic, C-C, C-halide or P-N bonds.
d) Lyases → Groups become removed (without hydrolysis) with the formation of double bonds
e) Isomerases → inter-conversion of optical, geometric or positional isomers.
f) Ligases → two compounds become linked (e.g. C-O, C-S, C-N, P-O etc. bonds.)

Cofactors

Cofactors are the non protein constituents of enzymes, which make it to become catalytically active. Apoenzyme is the protein pat of enzyme. Prosthetic groups, co enzymes and metal ions are the three kinds of cofactors.

a) Prosthetic groups (organic compounds) are tightly bound with apoenzymes. peroxidase and catalase (causes break down of H_2O_2 into water and oxygen). Haem is the part active site of enzyme.
b) Coenzymes (organic compounds) show transient association with apoenzymes. e.g. NAD, NADP

Metal ions form coordination bond at active site of end enzyme and responsible for one or more coordination bond with substrate. E.g. Zinc for carboxypeptidase (proteolytic enzymes).

A		B	
Components	**% of the total cellular mass**	**Proteins**	**Functions**
Water	70-90	Collagens	Intercellular ground substance
Proteins	10-15	Trypsin	Enzymes
Nucleic acids	5-7	Insulin	Hormone
Carbohydrates	3	Antibody	Fight infectious agents
Lipids	2	Receptors	Sensory reception like smell, taste, hormone etc.
Ions	1	GLUT-4	Enhance glucose transport into cells.

Table-3: (A) Average composition of cell, (B) Some proteins and their functions

DIFFERENCE BETWEEN:

Saturated fatty acid	Unsaturated fatty acid
1. It only contains single bonds in between carbon atoms.	1. It contains one or more double bonds in between carbon atoms.
2. It has straight chain structure.	2. Here chain is bent at double bond site.
3. It is the part of solid fat (like butter).	3. It is the part of liquid fat (like vegetable oil).

4. Its main source is animal fat. 5. Example: palmitic acid, Stearic acid.	4. Its main source is plant oil. 5. Example: Oleic acid, Lenoleic acid etc.
Triglycerides	**Phospholipids**
1. It is consisting of 1 glycerol and 3 fatty acids. 2. It is simple lipids. 3. It is non polar. 4. Main storage form of fat. 5. Example: fat and oil	1. It is consisting of 1 glycerol, 2 fatty acids and phosphate group. Here phosphate group attached to choline. 2. It is compound lipids. 3. It is amphipathic (polar head and nonpolar tail). 4. It is the component of cell membrane. 5. Example: Lecithin

KNOWLEDGE POINTS:

- ❖ Among 20 amino acids, almost all amino acids except glycine are asymmetric.
- ❖ Thousands of different proteins are present in cell and show different biological activity. Simple proteins only give amino acids on hydrolysis. In conjugated proteins, prosthetic group or metal are present along with amino acid.
- ❖ If amino acid sequence is changed then protein functions will be changed.
- ❖ In some proteins, protein structure is stabilized by non peptide covalent bond i.e. sulfide bond
- ❖ Tertiary structure is 3D structure of polypeptide. Many proteins are either fibrous and globular

MULTIPLE CHOICE QUESTIONS (MCQs)-1

1. Select the correct statement with reference to enzymes.
   (a) Holoenzyme = Coenzyme + Co-factor
   (b) Holoenzyme = Apoenzyme +Coenzyme

(c) Apoenzyme = Holoenzyme +Coenzyme
(d) Coenzyme = Apoenzyme + Holoenzyme

2. Which of the following is a non-proteinaceous enzyme ?
(a) deoxyribonuclease
(b) ligase
(c) Ribozyme
(d) lysozyme

3. Which of following is least likely to be involved in stabilizing the three-dimensional folding of most of the proteins?
(a) Hydrophobic interaction
(b) Electrostatic interaction
(c) Hydrogen bonds
(d) Ester bonds

4. Select the incorrect statement
(a) Sucrose is a disaccharide
(b) Uracil is a pyrimidine
(c) Glycine is a sulphur containing amino acid
(d) Cellulose is a polysaccharide

5. The chitinous exoskeleton of arthropods is formed by the polymerization of
(a) D-glucosamine
(b) lipoglycans
(c) N – acetyl glucosamine
(d) keratin sulphate and chondroitin sulphate

6. Which biomolecule has a phosphodiester bond ?
(a) fatty acids in a diglyceride
(b) amino acids in a polypeptide
(c) monosaccharides in a polysaccharide
(d) nucleic acids in a nucleotide

7. Find out incorrect statement with regards to enzyme action .
(a) Malonate is a competitive inhibitor of succinic dehydrogenase.
(b) Addition of lot of succinate does not reverse the inhibition of succinic dehydrogenase by malonate.
(c) Substrate binds with enzyme at its active site.
(d) a non-competitive inhibitor binds the enzyme at a site distinct from that which binds the substrate

8. Macromolecule chitin is consisting of _______.
(a) Nitrogen-containing polysaccharide.
(b) Phosphorous-containing polysaccharide.

(c) Sulphur containing polysaccharide.
(d) Simple polysaccharide

9. Select incorrect statement about enzymes.
   (a) Enzymes are highly specific.
   (b) Enzymes are denatured at high temperatures.
   (c) Enzymes require optimum pH and temperature for maximum activity.
   (d) Enzymes are mostly proteins but some are lipids also
10. Find correct statement about biomolecules.
   (a) Alanine amino acid – contains an amino group and an acidic group anywhere in the molecule
   (b) Palmitic acid – an unsaturated fatty acid with 18 carbon atoms
   (c) Lecithin – a phosphorylated glyceride found in the cell membrane
   (d) Adenylic acid – adenosine with a glucose phosphate molecule

MULTIPLE CHOICE QUESTIONS (MCQs)-2

1. Find out the wrong statement.
   (a) Sucrose is a disaccharide
   (b) Cellulose is a polysaccharide
   (c) Uracil is a pyrimidine
   (d) Glycine is a sulphur containing amino acid
2. A typical molecule is made up of:
   (a) Three glycerol molecules and one fatty acid molecule
   (b) One glycerol and three fatty acid molecules
   (c) One glycerol and one fatty acid molecule
   (d) Three glycerol and three fatty acid molecules
3. Which of the following is a non-proteinaceous enzyme?
   (a) Ribozyme
   (b) Ligase
   (c) Deoxyribonuclease
   (d) Lysozyme
4. Select incorrect option with respect to enzyme action.
   (a) Substrate binds with enzyme at its active site
   (b) Addition of lot of succinate does not reverse the inhibition of Succinic dehydrogenase by malonate

(c) A non – competitive inhibitor binds the enzyme at a site distinct from that which binds the substrate
(d) Malonate is a competitive inhibitor of Succinic dehydrogenase

5. Select non reducing carbohydrate?
   (a) Maltose
   (b) Sucrose
   (c) Lactose
   (d) Ribulose 5 – phosphate
6. Which one of the following statement is incorrect?
   (a) A competitive inhibitor reacts reversibly with the enzyme to form an enzyme inhibitor complex
   (b) In competitive inhibition, the inhibitor molecule is not chemically change by the enzyme
   (c) The competitive inhibitor does not affect the rate of breakdown of the enzyme subtract complex
   (d) The present of the competitive inhibitor decreases the Km of the enzyme for the substrate.
7. The transition state structure of the substrate formed during an enzymatic reaction is
   (a) Transient but stable
   (b) Permanent but unstable
   (c) Transient and unstable
   (d) Permanent and stable
8. A phosphoglyceride is always made up of
   (a) Only a saturated fatty acid esterified to a glycerol molecule to which a phosphate group is also attached.
   (b) Only an unsaturated fatty acid esterified to a glycerol molecule to which a phosphate group is also attached.
   (c) A saturated or unsaturated fatty acid esterified to a glycerol molecule to which a phosphate group is also attached.
   (d) A saturated or unsaturated fatty acid esterified to a phosphate group which is also attached to a glycerol molecule.
9. Select the correct statement:
   (a) Low temperature preserves the enzyme in a temporarily inactive state.
   (b) Higher temperature destroys enzymatic activity because proteins are denatured by heat.

(c) The activity of enzymes declines both below and above the optimum value.
(d) All of these

10. The essential chemical components of many coenzymes are
    (a) Proteins
    (b) Nucleic acids
    (c) Carbohydrates
    (d) Vitamins

ASSERTION AND REASON QUESTIONS:

Read the **assertion** *and* **reason** *carefully to mark the correct option out of the options given below:*

(a) If both the assertion and the reason are true and the reason is a correct explanation of the assertion.
(b) If both the assertion and reason are true but the reason is not a correct explanation of the assertion.
(c) If the assertion is true but the reason is false.
(d) If both the assertion and reason are false.

1. **Assertion:** The example of homo polymer is cellulose.
   Reason: Only one type of monosaccharide (glucose) are present in cellulose.
2. **Assertion:** The catalytic activity of enzymes depends upon co-factor.
   Reason: If co-factor is removed, catalytic activity will be lost.
3. **Assertion:** Biomolecules are present in living organism only.
   Reason: Only carbon atoms are the components of biomolecules.
4. **Assertion:** Nucleotides are present in DNA and RNA only
   Reason: The monomeric units of Nucleic acid are nucleotides.
5. **Assertion:** In acid soluble fraction, biomacromolecules are present.
   Reason: The molecular weight of biomacromolecules is less than 1000 dalton.
6. **Assertion:** The interaction between starch and I2 gives blue colour
   Reason: Starch has helical structure, so it can hold I2.
7. **Assertion:** The interaction between cellulose and I2 doesn't give colour.
   Reason: Cellulose cannot hold I2 due to absence of helix structure.
8. **Assertion:** The example of unsaturated fatty acid is arachidonic acid.

Reason: One or more than one double bonds are present in unsaturated fatty acids.

9. **Assertion:** Amino acids are amphoteric in nature.
   Reason: In our body, all amino acids are needed.
10. **Assertion:** Enzymes become inactive or incomplete in the absence of coenzyme (nonprotein group).
    Reason: Coenzymes provide attachment site for the chemical group and influence its properties.
11. **Assertion:** Enzyme **a**ctivity is depending on pH of medium.
    Reason: If pH of the medium is changed, then solubility of the enzyme in water will be affected.
12. **Assertion:** Prosthetic groups are the coenzymes or metal ions, which are very tightly bound to enzyme protein.
    Reason: Enzymes (catalytically active) along with prosthetic group is called apoenzyme.

***

Answer keys for
Multiple choice questions (MCQ) and Assertion and Reason questions

Chapter-1 : Animal Kingdom

MCQ-1

Q	1	2	3	4	5	6	7	8
A	c	d	d	d	d	a	b	d

MCQ-2

Q	1	2	3	4	5	6	7	8	9	10
A	d	c	a	d	a	c	c	b	d	c
Q	11	12	13	14	15					
A	a	b	c	c	c					

Assertion and Reasons

Q	1	2	3	4	5	6	7	8	9	10	11	12
A	a	c	a	d	c	a	c	a	c	b	a	d

Chapter-2: Structural organization in Animals

MCQ-1

Q	1	2	3	4	5	6	7	8	9	10
A	d	b	d	c	d	c	c	b	a	a

MCQ-2

Q	1	2	3	4	5	6	7	8	9	10
A	b	d	c	b	b	a	a	b	b	d
Q	11	12	13	14	15	16	17	18	19	20
A	d	d	a	a	c	a	c	c	b	b
Q	21	22	23	24	25					

A	b	c	a	c	b

MCQ-3

Q	1	2	3	4	5	6	7	8	9	10	11
A	c	d	a	b	c	c	d	a	d	a	c

Assertion and Reasons

Q	1	2	3	4	5	6	7	8	9	10	11	12
A	a	b	a	a	a	a	a	a	d	d	a	b

Chapter-3: Breathing and Exchange of gases

MCQ-1

Q	1	2	3	4	5	6	7	8	9	10	11	12
A	b	d	b	d	d	c	c	b	c	a	b	b

MCQ-2

Q	1	2	3	4	5	6	7	8	9	10
A	b	c	c	c	b	b	b	b	a	c

Assertion and Reasons

Q	1	2	3	4	5	6	7	8	9	10
A	c	a	d	a	a	d	d	c	b	c

Chapter-4: Body fluid and Circulation

MCQ-1

Q	1	2	3	4	5	6	7	8	9	10	11
A	c	d	d	b	c	a	c	a	a	c	a

MCQ-2

Q	1	2	3	4	5	6	7	8	9	10
A	a	d	d	a	a	d	d	b	b	c

Assertion and Reasons

Q	1	2	3	4	5	6	7	8	9	10
A	a	c	a	a	a	a	a	a	a	a

Chapter-5: Excretory products and its elimination

MCQ-1

Q	1	2	3	4	5	6	7	8	9
A	c	a	a	a	c	a	d	a	d

MCQ-2

Q	1	2	3	4	5	6	7	8	9	10
A	c	c	a	d	d	a	c	d	d	b

Assertion and Reasons

Q	1	2	3	4	5	6	7	8	9	10
A	a	c	a	c	a	b	a	a	a	a

Chapter-6: Locomotion and Movement

MCQ-1

Q	1	2	3	4	5	6	7	8	9
A	b	c	c	d	a	d	c	c	d

MCQ-2

Q	1	2	3	4	5	6	7	8	9	10
A	c	d	d	c	c	b	c	b	b	a

Assertion and Reasons

Q	1	2	3	4	5	6	7	8	9	10
A	a	c	b	a	a	a	a	a	a	b

Chapter-7: Neural control and coordination

MCQ-1

Q	1	2	3	4	5	6	7	8	9	10	11
A	a	d	a	c	b	c	c	a	a	c	b

Assertion and Reasons

Q	1	2	3	4	5	6	7	8	9	10
A	a	a	b	c	a	a	a	b	a	a

Chapter-8: Chemical Coordination and Integration

MCQ-1

Q	1	2	3	4	5	6	7	8	9	10
A	d	d	b	b	a	a	d	b	b	a

MCQ-2

Q	1	2	3	4	5	6	7	8	9	10
A	d	b	b	a	b	a	c	b	c	c
Q	11	12	13	14	15					
A	c	b	c	a	c					

Assertion and Reasons

Q	1	2	3	4	5	6	7	8	9	10	11
A	d	a	a	a	a	a	a	a	c	a	d

Chapter-9: Biomolecules

MCQ-1

Q	1	2	3	4	5	6	7	8	9	10
A	b	c	d	c	c	d	b	a	d	c

MCQ-2

Q	1	2	3	4	5	6	7	8	9	10
A	d	b	a	b	b	d	c	c	d	d

Assertion and Reasons

Q	1	2	3	4	5	6	7	8	9	10
A	a	a	d	c	d	a	a	a	c	a
Q	11	12								
A	b	c								

www.ingramcontent.com/pod-product-compliance
Ingram Content Group UK Ltd.
Pitfield, Milton Keynes, MK11 3LW, UK
UKHW021407190726
13845UKWH00028B/925

9 789334 413908